W9-BBE-023

JOSHUA DREAD

JOSHUA DREAD

LEE BACON

DELACORTE PRESS

Clifton Park - Halfmoon Public Library
475 Moe Road
Clifton Park, New York 12065

This is a work of fiction. Names, characters, places, and incidents either are the product of the author's imagination or are used fictitiously. Any resemblance to actual persons, living or dead, events, or locales is entirely coincidental.

Text copyright © 2012 by Lee Bacon
Jacket art and interior illustrations copyright © 2012 by Brandon Dorman

All rights reserved. Published in the United States by Delacorte Press,
an imprint of Random House Children's Books,
a division of Random House, Inc., New York.

Delacorte Press is a registered trademark and the colophon is a trademark of Random House, Inc.

Visit us on the Web! randomhouse.com/kids

Educators and librarians, for a variety of teaching tools, visit us at
RHTeachersLibrarians.com

Library of Congress Cataloging-in-Publication Data
Bacon, Lee.
Joshua Dread / Lee Bacon. — 1st ed.
p. cm.
Summary: Besides being bullied, Joshua faces one more obstacle in middle school, trying to hide his identity as the son of supervillains, the Dread Duo.
ISBN 978-0-385-74185-9 (hc) — ISBN 978-0-375-99027-4 (lib. bdg.)
ISBN 978-0-375-98721-2 (ebook)
[1. Supervillains—Fiction. 2. Superheroes—Fiction. 3. Identity—Fiction.
4. Middle schools—Fiction. 5. Schools—Fiction.] I. Title.
PZ7.B13446Jo 2013
[Fic]—dc23
2012003155

The text of this book is set in 12-point Cochin.

Book design by Trish Parcell

Printed in the United States of America

10 9 8 7 6 5 4 3 2 1

First Edition

Random House Children's Books
supports the First Amendment and celebrates the right to read.

3408

For Eva

1

For most people, the end of the world is a bad thing. For others, it's a career.

Our class got out of sixth period early the day my parents tried to flood the earth. Weather forecasts predicted massive hurricanes, tornadoes, thunderstorms, typhoons, monsoons, mud slides, and heavy winds.

"We are asking all students to make an orderly exit," Principal Sloane's voice boomed over the loudspeaker. "Please do not run, push, or form an angry mob on your way out. Buses are waiting outside."

My parents never actually came out and *told* me they were planning on flooding the world. But they'd dropped plenty of hints over the previous few weeks. Dad had spent every spare minute in the backyard tinkering with his new Weather Alterator machine. And that morning, Mom gave me a sly wink as I was leaving for school. "You might want to take an umbrella with you," she said, smiling as if she knew something I didn't.

Stepping into the hallway now, I joined the mass of other students. I listened to the rain and wind beating against the walls outside, the sound of hundreds of feet moving across the floor inside.

Everyone seemed pretty calm, considering the world was about to end.

The weather was chaotic. Wind lashed in every direction. Massive gray clouds swirled violently overhead. Bolts of lightning flashed across the sky. It looked like it was raining and snowing at the same time.

"Weird weather, huh?"

I turned and saw my best friend, Milton, standing behind me. Well, technically, he was my *only* friend. I'd known him for two years, ever since my parents and I had moved onto his street. Milton was tall and gangly, with arms and legs like sticks that had been loosely tied together. His sandy blond hair always poked up in the back.

"Did you hear what the weather forecast said this morning?" Milton asked.

"Yeah." I looked up at the churning clouds. "They're predicting that the storms will destroy civilization as we know it."

"And it's perfect timing too! Mrs. Lange was about to give us a quiz when class got dismissed."

We both stopped talking when a bone-rattling crash of thunder echoed across the landscape.

"Come on," I said when the thunder had ended. "Let's get onto the bus before it leaves without us."

Milton and I pushed against the wind until we found our bus and took a seat near the back. The weather outside worsened as we waited. The wind blew a stop sign past my window. The sky exploded with lightning.

Finally the bus rumbled into motion. Looking out the rain-splattered window, I could see trees shaking and power lines snapping loose. We passed an electronics store where the manager was fighting off a group of looters with a vacuum cleaner.

That morning, before the weather had taken a turn for the deadly, it had been a sunny fall day in Sheepsdale, one of the last really warm days of the year. Sheepsdale was a small town in upstate New York, nestled between a river and rolling green hills. Except for the occasional threat of apocalyptic doom, it was a pretty uneventful place to live.

When we reached downtown, the harsh weather suddenly stopped. It was as if we'd passed under an enormous invisible roof. There was no rain or wind. Everything looked absolutely still. A wall of gray clouds swirled around us. An eerie silence hung in the air.

My first thought was that we'd entered the eye of the storm. But then the bus lurched to a halt, and I realized what was going on.

My parents were floating in the intersection. They were holding a press conference.

It's embarrassing to run into your parents when you're with people from school, especially when your parents are about to destroy the planet.

Mom was drifting five feet above the ground on her hover scooter, wearing her usual uniform—a green one-piece armor body shield and black eye mask. Dad was drifting beside her on his own hover scooter. He was dressed in a dark gray jumpsuit, with blood-red gloves and boots. He was wearing a pair of massive silver goggles.

Dozens of reporters surrounded them, spilling out into the street with their cameras and microphones.

Kids crowded to one side of the school bus, pressing their faces against the glass to get a better look.

"I can't hear anything!" someone in the front yelled. "Open a window!"

All at once, twenty windows rattled down.

I ducked low, worried that my parents would notice me. Milton squeezed against my shoulder to get a better look.

"That's the Dread Duo!" His voice was full of fear and amazement.

"Is it?" I asked, trying to sound like I wasn't sure who they were. Like I hadn't just eaten breakfast with the Dread Duo seven hours earlier.

"There's the Botanist." Milton pointed at my mom. "She can control plants with her mind. And next to her is Dr. Dread. He wears those goggles because of his superpowered eyesight. They set a horde of zombies loose in Washington, D.C., last year. They tried to vaporize California with a death laser, but then it got blocked by Captain Justice. I can't believe they're actually *here*."

Milton went quiet as soon as Dr. Dread—my dad— began speaking to the gathered reporters.

"You may have noticed the sudden change in weather when you reached this intersection." He gestured to the wall of pounding rain and snow that surrounded the calm, clear area of downtown where our bus was stopped. "We have created a Vortex of Silence, which neutralizes the effects of the Weather Alterator within a fifty-foot radius of wherever we go. This Vortex of Silence will keep us safe and dry, even as the weather outside gets worse."

"And we assure you that it *will* get worse," my mom continued. "Much worse. Unless the government agrees to meet our demands, every continent on earth will be destroyed in"—she checked her watch—"less than four hours."

My parents did this kind of thing sometimes—death lasers, rampaging zombies, floods. I guess it was part of their job description. They were two of the most feared supervillains in the world. But that was only one part of who they were. As far as anyone in town knew, my mom was just an ordinary horticulture professor at the local junior college and my dad was a stay-at-home inventor. They had a regular house in a regular neighborhood on the outskirts of a regular little town. And they had a regular son.

In other words, *me*.

My name's Joshua Dread. Well, that's one of my names, anyway. I've gone by lots of them. My last name changes every time my parents pick up and move to another new town. Some kids have to make new friends when they move. I have to make up a whole new identity. But I can't tell you the name I go by now. It would be too dangerous—for me, and probably for you too.

The press conference was still going on. Reporters screamed questions to my parents.

"How can you expect the government to meet such an unreasonable demand in such a short amount of time?" yelled one.

"I don't think a private jet filled with hundred-dollar bills is so unreasonable." A wicked smirk passed over my dad's face. "I prefer to think of it as . . . *creative*."

"What about Captain Justice?" called another reporter. "Aren't you concerned that he'll put a stop to these plans?"

My mom glared at the reporter with a sour expression. Captain Justice was the most famous superhero in the world. He was also my parents' archrival. Just mentioning his name around the house was enough to get me sent to my room.

"Actually," Mom said, "Captain Justice doesn't concern us. It's you who should be worried. All of you. Because soon—"

She was interrupted by a booming voice in the distance.

"DID SOMEONE SAY 'JUSTICE'?"

A flurry of excitement passed over the reporters. One of them pointed to the other side of the intersection, where a figure had appeared from the storm, floating above the rooftops, flying in our direction. I recognized him right away. I'd seen him in countless commercials and on magazine covers. He was wearing a tight silver jumpsuit and a shiny blue cape. His teeth were blindingly bright as he smiled.

Captain Justice had just arrived.

2

**If you're going to get into a deadly fight,
make sure you do it on camera.**

Milton pressed closer to me, trying to get a
better look. For as long as I'd known him,
he'd been obsessed with superheroes and supervillains,
but he'd been especially obsessed with Captain Justice. Milton had Captain Justice posters on his wall
and Captain Justice trading cards. The only cereal he
would eat was Frosted Fuel Flakes (sponsored by Captain Justice).

And now Captain Justice was floating just outside the
window.

"If it isn't the Botanist and Dr. Dread." Captain

Justice's voice echoed across downtown Sheepsdale. "How unpleasant it is to see you again."

My parents glared back at him.

"How did he get here so soon?" Dad muttered to Mom.

My dad's hand dropped down to his waist, his fingers running over a small gray box that was hanging from his belt. The control box for the Weather Alterator. It contained a button that could trigger total meteorological meltdown, destroying the world—or at least everything outside the Vortex of Silence—in a matter of seconds. And nobody, not even Captain Justice, could stop it.

"You are a truly wicked pair," Captain Justice said. "Flooding the earth. Terrorizing a group of journalists. Holding innocent children hostage. Is there any act of treachery that is too evil for the Dread Duo?"

My dad glanced at our school bus as if he hadn't noticed it until now. "We aren't holding any children hostage!"

"Silence! I didn't come here to listen to your pitiful excuses." Captain Justice turned to our bus. "Worry not, dear children! Captain Justice shall rescue you from the clutches of these vile enemies!"

Swooping downward, he gripped the bus roof. A wrenching sound filled the air as he tore the top half of the bus off. Some kids screamed. Milton snapped a photo with his cell phone.

"Be free, children!" Captain Justice said, holding the

top half of the bus above his head with one hand as if it weighed nothing at all. "You are trapped in this bus of death no longer!"

My classmates remained in their seats, stunned.

"Go on," Captain Justice urged. "You're all free now."

"Captain Justice?" said a girl a few rows ahead of me.

"What is it, little girl?"

"The bus driver said it wasn't safe for us to go outside the Vortex of Silence on foot. Because of the storm and all."

Captain Justice glanced up at the top half of the bus like he was trying to figure out whether he could reattach it.

"Never fear," he said. "Captain Justice will find a way for you to return to your homes safely."

He shrugged and then tossed the top of the bus over his shoulder like a crumpled piece of paper. The enormous metal object crashed into the post office, destroying the entire front wall.

I watched my dad with a rising sense of fear. He looked panicked, on the verge of pressing the meltdown button. I wished that they'd never gone ahead with this plan in the first place. What were we even supposed to *do* with a private jet full of hundred-dollar bills? Our driveway was barely big enough for my parents' Volvo.

I thought about calling out to them. Maybe I could convince my parents to give up their scheme and let everyone go. But what if someone realized that I was related to them? What if everyone in school found out that I was the son of the Dread Duo?

On second thought, I was better off taking my chances with world annihilation.

The weather continued to worsen. The tumble of clouds turned from gray to black. Rain lashed the sides of buildings; wind ripped street signs loose. But everything within fifty feet of our bus was perfectly calm and still.

Captain Justice had turned his back on my parents and was now floating ten feet off the ground, posing for photographs. He smiled at the crowd of journalists, flexing his muscles for the cameras.

My dad's finger inched closer to the meltdown button. I ducked even lower in my seat as he glanced at our bus. His eyes lingered on the bus for a split second, and then he shook his head and pulled his hand away from the button. He reached for another part of his utility belt. His plasma gun.

"Hey, Captain Justice," he said, removing the gun from its holster. "How about one more shot?"

He aimed and pulled the trigger. A vivid red beam burst out of the end of the gun.

Captain Justice spun around, yelling, "Engage Shield of Honor!"

A glowing blue shield took form in Captain Justice's

hand. It looked both real and unreal, like a hologram had emerged from his wristband. The plasma beam reflected off the Shield of Honor and hit Mom's hover scooter. She crashed to the ground.

Dad flew over to help her just as Captain Justice raised his other hand. "Engage Net of Truth!"

Another blue hologram appeared from his wristband. This time it looked like a net, which flew just over our heads and collided with my father. He and his hover scooter crashed into a bush.

"You see that, kids?" Captain Justice said, drifting closer to our school bus. "This just goes to show that honor and truth always prevail. It reminds me of the time I single-handedly battled Abominator and his army of mutants. They had me surrounded, but I was able to—OOF!"

Captain Justice's speech came to a sudden halt as the branches of a nearby tree circled around his waist. Before he could escape the tree's grip, it whipped forward, flinging him through the air like a superhero-shaped football. He soared over the top of our bus and past the crowd of journalists before crashing into a Chinese food restaurant at the corner.

Now, some people might find it slightly unusual to see plants go on the attack like that. But when your mom can control any kind of vegetation on earth, you get used to it.

Dad untangled himself from the hologram net and launched across the intersection on his hover scooter. At the other end of the street, Captain Justice was lying in a pile of rubble and egg rolls. Dad fired his plasma gun.

ZAAAAP!

Everyone around me gasped, then cheered as Captain Justice dove to the side. The plasma beam flew over his shoulder, igniting a box of fortune cookies behind him.

Captain Justice was on his feet in an instant.

"Engage Spear of Freedom!" His voice boomed through downtown Sheepsdale as he thrust a hologram spear into the air.

Dad veered to the side, and the spear grazed his utility belt, causing an explosion of sparks.

All at once, a remarkable change took place around me. The sky changed from dark gray to mild blue. The rain that had been pounding the scenery outside the Vortex of Silence vanished. Sunlight reflected in the puddles on the nearby streets.

Downtown Sheepsdale had returned to a normal sunny afternoon.

Dad glanced up at the sky, disappointment and rage filling his features. "Curse you, Captain Justice! You destroyed the remote for the Weather Alterator. It took me six months to construct that!"

Captain Justice looked just as surprised as my parents. "That's—er . . . exactly what I intended to do." He puffed out his chest as his beaming smile returned.

Dad was still lying on the ground gripping his ankle. His expression turned from anger to fear as Captain Justice grabbed a huge chunk of the wall that had once belonged to the Chinese restaurant.

"And now, to finish you off . . ." Captain Justice raised the section of the wall above his head, taking aim.

"WAIT!"

It took me a second to realize that I'd been the one to call out. Everyone on the bus turned to look at me. I hoped that my face didn't look as red as it felt.

"Yes, child?" Captain Justice was grinning at me, waiting for me to say something.

My mind spun. I'd only yelled to distract him from killing my parents—I hadn't really put much thought into what I should say after that.

I caught a glimpse of my dad lying on the ground. Recognition flashed across his features. He looked as if he couldn't figure out whether to wave hello or scream for mercy. Everyone was watching me—Captain Justice, my parents, dozens of reporters. I shielded my eyes from the glare of flashing cameras, then cleared my throat.

"Um . . . would it—" My voice sputtered and I tried again. "Would it be possible to take a picture of you?"

"Oh, okay." Captain Justice grinned. "Maybe just one photo."

Floating in place, the superhero fixed his hair with one hand and balanced the brick wall above his head with the other.

The distraction was enough for Dad to get out his plasma gun. With a blast of red light, the brick wall exploded into a million pieces.

Captain Justice covered his eyes as dust from the destroyed wall rained down on him. Smoke from the explosion hung in the air. Dad aimed the plasma gun at Captain Justice's chest.

"No!" I screamed.

I could see the hesitation on Dad's face. His greatest enemy was floating in front of him, blinded. All he had to do was pull the trigger. He glanced from Captain Justice to me. With a sigh, he grabbed his hover scooter and flew to where Mom was lying. After helping her onto his scooter, Dad turned to give Captain Justice one last dirty look. Then my parents rose high into the air together. A moment later, they were gone.

When Captain Justice could see again, he flew toward us, brushing dust and brick fragments out of his hair.

"Another shameful plot has been foiled by Captain Justice!" he said, among wild whoops and cheers from the crowd of students and journalists. "But we must all remain diligent. For we never know when evil will strike again. One thing is certain, though. If you want to grow up to be super like me, you'll remember to eat Frosted Fuel Flakes every morning for breakfast. Eight essential vitamins and all the nutrients you need to get your day started right!"

And then he launched into the air, vanishing into the blue, cloudless sky.

3

**Having superpowered parents
can make life complicated at times.**

The mood around the dining room table was tense. Mom was still wearing her body armor, but she'd slung her mask over the back of the chair and replaced her knee-high black boots with white slippers. Dad pushed his goggles onto his forehead and stared at his plate of salmon and asparagus as if it had just insulted him.

"What is it with that doofus always flying in and foiling our schemes?" he said. "I can't even destroy one stupid little continent without him getting in the way!"

"And what's the deal with all those hologram weapons?" Mom said. "The Net of Truth! The Shield of Glory!"

"Honor," I said. "It was actually called the Shield of—"

Mom glared over at me. I decided it might not be the best time to dwell on specifics.

"Never mind," I said.

The TV was playing in the living room, a jumble of noise in the background. Dad stabbed a bunch of asparagus with his fork like he was spearing a whale with a harpoon.

When the local news started, both of them turned to face the television. A reporter was standing on a street that looked familiar, pointing toward a pile of rubble that also looked familiar. Nearby was half a school bus that definitely looked familiar. It was the scene of the fight between my parents and Captain Justice.

"Today's top story," said the reporter. "Shock in Sheepsdale, as two supervillains tried to destroy the world by altering the weather."

I cleared my throat. "You know what would be nice? Family dinner without TV."

If my parents were in a bad mood now, the news was only going to make it worse. But it was too late. They were already shifting in their seats to get a better view of the television.

The reporter continued. "I'm standing outside what's left of Mr. Chow's Chinese Buffet in downtown

Sheepsdale. But the only thing on the menu today was chaos, as the Dread Duo frightened a busful of children. According to eyewitness accounts, the Botanist ripped a school bus in half while it was still full of students from Sheepsdale Middle School."

"I didn't do that!" Mom yelled at the screen. "Captain Justice tore that bus apart! I mean, I appreciate the credit, but—"

"Afterward," the reporter went on, "she threw the top half of the school bus at a nearby post office."

Mom shook her head with frustration.

"Fortunately, Captain Justice came to the rescue," the reporter said. "While fighting against the two dastardly supervillains, the beloved Captain Justice single-handedly saved the school children and put a halt to a plot to destroy the world. If there's one thing we can agree on, it's that Captain Justice is a true superhero.

"After a short break, we'll take it to Troy, who's going to tell us more about that wacky weather today!"

Since it didn't look like the world was going to be destroyed after all, I still had some homework to finish after dinner.

Most people imagine that supervillains live in

hollowed-out volcanoes or secret arctic lairs. But our house looked just like everyone else's. When your family has a secret identity, it's not a good idea to draw attention to yourself by installing death satellites or converting the garage into a dungeon.

But if you'd looked closer, you might have noticed the little details that made our house different from the others. Like the extra-tall fence in the backyard that blocked any view of what my parents were working on back there. Or the network of invisible sensor beams that formed a security perimeter around all the doors and windows. Or the curtains on our basement windows that hid the zombies my mom kept locked down there.

I walked past the closed door to my parents' lab, where they plotted out most of their evil plans. I paused to glance at my reflection in the hall mirror. Mom and Dad kept assuring me that I would be hitting a growth spurt any day now, but so far all I'd hit was a growth sputter. I still could barely see myself in the bottom of the mirror. Disheveled brown hair, a constellation of pale freckles scattered across my nose.

For the next couple of hours, I stuck to my bedroom. I'd had enough experience with these types of situations to know that it was best to just avoid my parents until they'd recovered from their foul mood. By the next day, they'd be over their disappointment again.

When I headed back downstairs for a glass of water,

it was so quiet that I thought they'd gone to bed. But I heard whispers coming from the living room.

"Don't you think it's time we tell him?" Dad asked.

"Not yet," Mom replied. "Let's just wait a little longer. He's still young."

"He deserves to know."

Mom sighed. "You're right, Dominick. I'm just worried about him, that's all."

I peered around the doorway. My parents were seated on the couch. The television was muted. The light from the screen flickered over my dad's features as he leaned forward and rubbed his temples.

"Joshua is going to find out soon, you know," he said. "Whether we tell him or not, he'll discover the truth."

"Soon," Mom said. "We'll tell him soon. But not yet. Give him just a little more time."

What were they talking about? What did I deserve to know? Before I could get any answers, Captain Justice appeared on TV in a commercial for Pegasus shoes. Quick shots of him running, lifting weights, practicing with holographic nunchucks—all while wearing Pegasus shoes.

Dad grabbed his plasma gun and pulled the trigger. The TV disintegrated.

When household accessories started getting vaporized, that usually meant it wasn't the best time for a chat. I turned and tiptoed back upstairs.

The next morning, I climbed out of bed and headed into the bathroom. On the wall beside the sink was a silver box with the words "No Handz WonderBrush" printed in the center. This was one of Dad's inventions. See, when my dad wasn't busy inventing devious technologies to terrorize the planet, he spent his time inventing devious technologies that terrorized the rest of the family.

His inventions weren't supposed to be dangerous. It was just that Dad was an impatient guy. Mom accused him of having SADD (Supervillain Attention Deficit Disorder). He'd start on one project, then get another idea and get all carried away with something else, until a new plan gripped his imagination, and another, and . . . you get the idea.

Because of Dad's SADD, our house was stuffed with inventions that he was too distracted to ever quite finish. Some of his ideas were pretty cool. But a lot of them were also kind of life-threatening.

Like the No Handz WonderBrush.

"This little device makes brushing your teeth easier than ever before!" Dad had explained to me while installing the prototype in my bathroom the previous year. I'd considered mentioning that brushing my teeth wasn't actually all that hard to begin with, but he'd been caught up in his explanation. He'd pressed a button, and a mechanical arm had swung out of the wall with a toothbrush attached to the end. "See?" he'd said. "Easy. Now just relax while the No Handz brushes your teeth for you!"

That was the idea, anyway. The one time I tried it, the No Handz ended up brushing my eyeballs. Since then, I've stuck with my normal toothbrush.

And it's not like Mom made my life any easier. She was constantly testing out her experiments around the house. That morning was no exception. When I got downstairs for breakfast, she was placing a small potted tree on the floor next to the dining room table.

"What does this look like?" she asked, pointing at the tree.

It had to be a trick question. "Um . . . a tree?" I said.

"It's actually a genetically engineered mutant ficus," she said.

See what I mean? Trick question.

"I've been working in the lab on this for months. And I think it's finally ready." Mom turned and faced the tree. "Well, are you ready?"

She was speaking to the tree. And that wasn't even the weirdest part. Because a second later, the tree flapped forward and back several times. Like a nod.

"Did you make it do that?" I asked.

"Nope," Mom said. "Micus did that all on his own."

"Micus?"

"Mutant Ficus. He's been genetically engineered to understand human language by measuring the vibration in our voices. And he's also capable of responding to simple questions and expressing himself."

The tree seemed to be looking up at Mom now. Its branches flapped up and down like arms.

"So, uh—what does it want now?" I asked.

Mom examined the tree. "At the moment, he appears to be hungry?"

Micus nodded more enthusiastically than the previous time.

"Would you like to feed him?" Mom asked.

The tree turned in my direction. Strange that you could feel like you were being watched by something without eyes.

"Go ahead," Mom said. "Micus won't bite. Will you, Micus?"

The tree shook its bushy head back and forth.

"That's okay," I said. "Actually, there was something else I wanted to talk to you about."

All morning, questions had been swimming through my head. What had my parents been whispering about the night before? What were they keeping from me?

But this obviously wasn't the time to ask. Mom was distracted by Micus, who'd begun flailing his branches around like a little kid throwing a temper tantrum.

"Oh, now he's upset. Here, give him some of this." Mom

pushed a plastic jug into my hands. Water sloshed around inside. "A little water ought to make him feel better."

"Are you sure?" I asked.

"Absolutely. Once he has something to drink, he'll perk right up."

"Okay." Leaning forward, I tilted the jug. All of a sudden, Micus wrapped a branch around my wrist. I tried to pull back, but Micus was surprisingly strong for a houseplant.

"No, Micus!" Mom yelled. "Let go of Joshua at once!"

Instead, the tree pulled my wrist down. Water gushed out of the jug, landing in the pot and spilling over the edges.

"Okay, I'll give you what you want!" I screamed. "Just don't hurt me!"

I couldn't believe it had come to this—bargaining for my life with a potted tree. Micus yanked harder, and the rest of the water came splashing out of the jug. Finally Mom raised her hand, palm out. She stared hard at the tree, a concentrated expression that always showed up on her face when she used her power. I felt the plant's grip loosening. As soon as I was free, I leaped around to the other end of the dining room table to catch my breath.

Maybe I wasn't in the mood for breakfast after all.

When I got to school, everyone was talking about the fight between Captain Justice and my parents. A You-Tube video of my dad getting caught in the Net of Truth had gone viral overnight. Things only got worse on my way to third period. I was rounding a corner near the main stairway when a harsh voice called out to me.

"Hey, Dorkface! Where ya going?"

My stomach did a somersault. The voice belonged to Joey Birch. As for "Dorkface"—well, I guess that was another of the names I went by.

Joey was wiry and tall, with red hair and pale, sharp features. He roamed the hallways of Sheepsdale Middle School threatening, stealing, bribing, cheating—followed everywhere by Brick Gristol.

Nobody knew how Brick had gotten his nickname. Maybe it had something to do with his level of intelligence. Or maybe it was because his head was as flat and hard as a brick. There were rumors that he'd been held back three times. This would have explained why he was the only kid in the sixth grade who had a five o'clock shadow and a learner's permit.

Brick grinned down at me, showing off a mouthful of crooked teeth. He was wearing a T-shirt that read:

This Shirt Is Made from
100%
Recycled Puppies

"Listen up, Dorkface," Joey said, taking a step in my direction. "We're trying to settle a little bet. Brick says that we could stuff you into a locker and shut the door. But I say we'd have to break your legs before you'd fit. Whaddaya think?"

Neither option sounded all that good to me, but I had a feeling that they weren't really asking for my advice. Besides, every time I tried to speak, the enormous knot in my throat got in the way, and I ended up making a sound that was something between a squeak and a gurgle.

"Here's what we'll do," Joey said. "Just break *one* of your legs and stuff you inside. If you don't fit, we'll break the other one."

Brick grabbed my arm with one hairy-knuckled hand. With his other hand, he reached out and yanked the knob of a nearby locker. The door swung open with a clang.

I could tell there was no way I was going to fit inside the locker. Not even close. I'd admit that I was kind of small for my age, but I was not nearly as bendable as I looked. I tried to mention this to Joey and Brick, but when I opened my mouth, I sounded like a suffocating hamster.

I glanced down at Brick's hand. It looked about the size of a catcher's mitt against my scrawny arm.

Brick pulled me closer to the locker.

"I hope you're flexible," Joey said. "'Cause it's gonna be a tight squeeze."

I can't really explain what happened next because I didn't understand it myself. But a weird feeling came over me. It started as a tingling in my fingertips and spread down my arms and across my pounding chest. Then a surge of energy pulsed through me, a rush of intense power bursting through my veins.

All of a sudden, Brick flew backward like he'd just been hit by an invisible eighteen-wheeler. A crash echoed through the hallway as he slammed into a row of lockers.

Joey looked from Brick to me, his eyes wide with shock. "How did you . . . ," he muttered. "That's not possible. . . ."

For once, Joey and I were in complete agreement. My brain buzzed with confusion. Somehow I'd just knocked the biggest kid in school into a locker without even raising a finger.

4

**It's perfectly normal
to feel strange and different.**

Over the previous few months, there'd been other instances like this. Weird, unexplained events happening around me. Like when I'd been in the middle of a math test and my pencil had exploded in my hand. Or the time, a couple of weeks after that, when I'd been on the floor playing a video game and I'd felt something burning. Dropping the controller, I'd scrambled to my feet. That was when I noticed the burn mark in the carpet right where I'd been sitting. And it had been shaped exactly like my butt.

Our health teacher had told us that our bodies

MILTON

Joshua's best friend and neighbor, Milton,
is a huge fan of Captain Justice...
and curly fries. Just watch out
when he gets too close to a hover scooter.

would be "experiencing many strange and wonderful changes."

For some reason, I didn't think this was what she'd had in mind.

I spent the next couple of periods in a daze. Something weird was going on, and I needed to figure out what it was.

During lunch, I sat down at an empty table and tried to re-create the surge of power I'd felt earlier. I shut out all the noises around me and strained my concentration. At first nothing happened. But then I felt it. A slight tingle in my fingertips. My heart pounded as a buzz of energy spread down my arms, and then—

"Are you okay? You look like you just swallowed a bug."

Milton set down his lunch tray beside me. All the focus fizzled away. I wasn't even sure that I'd felt anything at all.

"Hey, Milton," I said.

With his mouth half full of macaroni and cheese, Milton launched into a detailed replay of the fight between my parents and Captain Justice. "And the way Captain Justice destroyed the remote device with his Spear of Freedom!" Milton heaved a forkful of macaroni like it was a holographic spear. "Did you see Dr. Dread's face when the weather suddenly got better? He looked like such an idiot!"

I didn't know how much more of this I could take. It was bad enough I had to listen to my parents get insulted on the evening news and in the hallway of my school. Now I was hearing it from my best friend too.

But what was I supposed to do? I couldn't exactly go around defending the Dread Duo.

Suddenly Milton stopped talking. Looking up, I realized what had caught his attention. The Cafeteria Girls had just sat down at the other end of our table.

There were four of them. Seventh graders. Pretty in a too-much-makeup kind of way. They'd been sharing a table with us for the past two months (not that they'd ever noticed us), and somewhere along the way Milton and I had begun calling them the Cafeteria Girls (not that we ever told them that). They immediately launched into their usual activity—criticizing everyone in sight.

"Check out Jenny Allen's haircut!"

"Is that a pimple, or is James Wendler growing a second head?"

"Look at Maria Rodriguez's shoes! What did she do? Steal them from a homeless astronaut?"

They went on like this for the next ten minutes or so, commenting on the clothing, appearance, and grooming habits of everyone who passed through the cafeteria. Sitting so close to them gave Milton and me access to all the gossip and trash talk Sheepsdale Middle School had to offer.

"Who's the new girl?" One of the girls pointed across the cafeteria at someone I'd never seen before.

"Sophie Smith. Sixth grader."

"Did you hear what Daniel Clark said about her?"

The rest of the Cafeteria Girls shook their heads.

"Daniel's older brother works for a moving company that helped Sophie Smith and her dad move into this, like, castle outside town. She doesn't have a mom. No brothers or sisters either. Just the two of them in this enormous house. And the stuff they were moving. He'd never seen anything like it before."

"What kind of stuff?"

Lowering her voice, the girl telling the story leaned across the table. The others did the same. Milton and I craned our necks to listen.

"Weird stuff," she whispered. "They had three entire moving vans full of flat-screen TVs. At least two hundred of them. And there were other things too. One truck was full of boxes that were completely empty. I mean, who brings an entire truck full of empty boxes?"

Taking a bite of my sandwich, I couldn't help wondering if any of this was actually true. Out of the corner of my eye, I saw Milton sipping his chocolate milk and trying to listen without seeming conspicuous.

"Wanna know the craziest thing, though?" The girl paused long enough to snap her gum. "Outside the house, there were guard towers. With machine guns."

The entire table gasped. Milton spit out his milk.

Luckily the Cafeteria Girls were too immersed in the story to notice.

"Machine guns? Why?"

"That's the point. Nobody knows. So I'm thinking that Sophie Smith is the daughter of, like, some mob boss who really likes TV or maybe a superwealthy guy who collects weird stuff for no reason and worries a lot about security, or maybe—"

"Shhh. Here she comes."

The table went silent. I snuck a glance at Sophie as she passed our table. Light swam in her blue-gray eyes. Holding her food tray with one hand, she pushed a strand of blond hair out of her face with the other.

She scanned the room, looking for a place to sit. For a second I felt sorry for her. First day in a new school without any friends. I'd been there before.

I was about to offer Sophie a seat at our table—it would have been worth it just to see the looks on the Cafeteria Girls' faces. But before I could say anything, she turned and walked outside.

Rumors spread about Sophie Smith like a bad case of acne. People said that her dad was a celebrity in hiding. That she'd spent the last several years in an exclusive private school for the children of powerful parents. That she was an antisocial weirdo. That she only talked to the kids of other famous people. That her dad moved to Sheepsdale to get away from the paparazzi . . .

But in the end, they were just rumors. Sophie and her father were a mystery. A mystery everyone in school seemed to know about.

When I got to seventh period, I took a seat at the back of the room. Joey and Brick were at their usual desks in the middle of the class (the most beneficial spot for cheating purposes). As soon as I sat down, they turned around in their desks and stared at me. I tried to block them out, but that wasn't so easy.

"I think Joey and Brick are trying to get your attention," Milton said, poking me on the shoulder.

"I know that, Milton." I focused on my desk. "I'm ignoring them."

"Brick just rolled up his sleeves, and now he's staring at you as he pounds his fist against the table."

"Thanks for the commentary."

"And Joey's superangry about something. Looks like he's writing a note. Hmm. I wonder what it says. Okay, he's folding the note and passing it to Jade Watkins. Now she's passing it over to Sam Berthold, and he's passing it to . . . Oh— Hold on a second."

Sam handed the note to Milton, who took one look at it, then tapped me on the shoulder.

"It's for you." Milton dropped the note on my desk.

I unfolded the sheet of paper and glanced down at Joey's sloppy handwriting.

Dear Dorkface,
    You = Dead Meat.
    From,
    Joey and Brick
P.S. Tell Milton to shut up.

I looked up from the note when I heard a wave of whispers sweep across the classroom. Sophie Smith had entered through the doorway. The entire class watched as she crossed the room. Even Joey and Brick.

Sophie passed between the rows of desks toward the back of the room, where Milton and I were sitting.

"Is this seat taken?" She pointed to an empty seat beside me.

I stared back at her, thinking about all the things I'd heard. The trucks full of TVs and empty boxes, the machine guns—

"No," I blurted out. "I mean—yes."

Sophie tilted her head.

"What I mean is that, *no*, this seat isn't taken, and *yes*, you can sit down," I finally got out.

"Thanks."

And then she did.

Seventh period was American history. Our teacher was Ms. McGirt, who was somewhere between seventy and seven hundred years old. She had a fluff of white hair and a pair of eyes that were magnified behind thick glasses.

Ms. McGirt was half blind and three-fourths deaf. She misunderstood whenever students asked questions, she didn't notice us raising our hands, and she never caught Joey and Brick cheating off the students around them. All of this made class interesting for reasons that had nothing to do with American history.

As the bell rang, Ms. McGirt rose from her desk, wobbled across the room, and began to describe our class project.

"It will have a specific emphasis on DNLS—Date, Name, Location, Significance." She spoke in a high, shaky voice, blinking at the class in front of her as if she weren't sure we were even there. "If you can adequately recite the DNLS of a historic event, then you will come away with a superb comprehension of American history. Is that understood?"

"No," Joey said.

"Very good. Let's continue."

Brick laughed. Ms. McGirt, oblivious, went on.

"Students will organize themselves into groups of

three," she said. "Each group will prepare a ten-minute presentation."

The class let out a collective groan. Ms. McGirt ignored this (probably because she didn't hear it).

"Your assignment is to choose a specific historic event and focus on DNLS," she said. "Who can tell me what these letters stand for again?"

"Dumb Nut Loser School?" Joey said.

"That is correct. Date, Name, Location, Significance. Now, please select your groups."

I already knew Milton and I would be in a group together. Turning in my desk, I looked around for a third person. Sophie's eyes caught mine.

"Would you—" I stopped myself. The gossip was swirling around in my head again. She was some rich celebrity's daughter; she lived in a giant house surrounded by machine guns; she only hung out with other kids of famous people. Why would someone like that want to partner up with a kid who goes by the name Dorkface?

"Sure! I'll work with you guys." Sophie smiled at me. "By the way, I'm Sophie. Sophie—Smith."

I gripped my desk a little tighter. Maybe it was just my imagination, but there was something strange about the way she'd said her first and last names. As if she couldn't quite remember how they fit together. After years of hiding my identity, I could recognize when someone was doing the same thing.

5

Sometimes it's best to turn to your parents for advice. They might know more about your situation than you think.

"**E**verything okay?" Dad asked. "You've been staring at your textbook for the past two minutes like it's written in binary."

He was holding a pair of his silver goggles in one hand and a tiny screwdriver in the other. Thanks to his superpowered eyesight, he could examine atomic particles without a microscope, and read fine print from a mile away. The goggles he'd invented allowed him to regulate his vision. They also looked intimidating and masked his identity. Perfect for the supervillain who wanted to be terrifying *and* practical.

"What's going on?" Dad asked, sitting on the couch beside me.

"Just something that happened at school today," I began. "These bullies—"

"Bullies?"

I stared at the floor. "Yeah."

"That's the problem with this world." Dad let out an angry sigh. "The big and powerful think they can push around the little guy. It's a vicious cycle. The bullies exploit the weak, and it makes them even stronger. Unless someone stands up to them. Unless someone fights back. Like your mom and I do."

"Um . . . okay, but—"

"See, that's the thing people don't understand about your mom and me," Dad went on. "*Sure,* we put on uniforms, and, *yes,* we threaten the government with total annihilation. But we're not out to destroy the world just for the sake of destroying it."

I wasn't sure what any of this had to do with my problem, but I nodded anyway.

"Our goal is to start the world over again. Reboot. Do it right the next time. Shake up the power structure. Of course, we need money for all that. Which is why it's necessary for us to make our little requests."

"You call a private jet full of hundred-dollar bills a *little request?*"

Dad shrugged. He gave the goggles a twist. The goggles let out a squeak.

"So did you stand up to these bullies?" he asked. "Did you show them that just because they're big and powerful, they can't get away with pushing around the little guy?"

"Not exactly. They tried to shove me into a locker."

"Hmm. Never gonna change the power structure that way."

"But something happened while they were trying to get me into the locker. This weird feeling came over me. And that's what I wanted to ask you about. It was like—"

"I have an idea."

"Huh?"

"An idea. For dealing with these jerks."

"That's okay. I actually was more curious about this other thing. The weird feeling."

"You can't run away, Joshua. You have to stand up for yourself."

I took a deep breath. There was no point in trying to explain myself to him. Not when he was swept up in his *big idea.*

"Fine," I said, crossing my arms. "What's your idea?"

"The next time you see these bullies, go up to the biggest guy and punch him in the nose. Then run as fast as you can. By the time they realize what happened, you'll be long gone."

Dad nodded once, as if he'd just handed down a piece of great wisdom.

"Uh, okay," I said. "But, Dad? When Brick grabbed my arm, I felt this—I don't know how to describe it—this powerful surge of—"

"Joshua!" My mom was standing in the doorway. "You can't allow yourself to be intimidated by bullies. Whether it's kids in school or governmental agencies."

"Yeah," I said. "I'll definitely keep that in mind. But I wanted to tell you that—"

"I'm sorry, but it'll have to wait," Mom interrupted. "I just came up to get some food for the zombies. And you know how zombies get when they haven't been fed. You can tell us all about your problem over dinner. Okay, honey?"

I was on my way into the dining room when a green arm reached out to grab me.

"Agh!" I screamed, jumping backward. It wasn't an arm at all. It was a branch.

Micus.

"What's *he* still doing here?" I yelled.

"Where else would he be?" Mom asked innocently. "We're in the house, and Micus is a *house*plant."

"A houseplant that tried to kill me this morning!"

43

"Micus didn't try to *kill* you. Did you, Micus?"

I couldn't be sure, but it looked to me like the tree shrugged.

"Can't we at least put him in another room?" I asked. "Your lab or something?"

"There's no direct sunlight in the lab."

"I'm sure he can handle that."

"Joshua! I spent months developing Micus. He's a biological breakthrough."

I noticed Micus nodding proudly in the background while she said this.

Dropping down into the seat at the table that was farthest from Micus, I shook my head in disbelief. First I got attacked by a potted tree. Then my mom took *his* side.

During dinner, I finally got a chance to tell my parents what had happened at school. While Dad served spaghetti, I described the tingling in my fingertips, the feeling of electricity that pulsed through my body.

"I think I might've shocked this kid so bad that he flew into a locker," I said.

My parents stared at me. A noodle slipped off the spoon my dad was holding. It landed on the table next to my plate.

"And that's not all," I said. "Other weird things have happened lately."

"What kinds of things?" Mom asked.

I took a deep breath. "Lately I've been accidentally causing stuff to . . . explode."

Another noodle landed on the table with a wet *splat*.

"Explode?"

I nodded.

"How long has this been going on?" Dad asked.

"Just the last few months."

Dad scratched his head. "Well, you *are* at the age when—"

He stopped speaking when Mom cleared her throat loudly.

"Perhaps it's best if we discuss this some other time," she said.

I pushed my plate aside. "What are you hiding from me?" My voice came out louder than I'd intended. "I know there's something going on. I heard you talking about it last night."

"You heard us?" Mom asked.

"You said there was something you needed to tell me. Something I deserve to know."

Mom sighed. "We wanted to tell you, but we also wanted to wait for the right time."

"It's perfectly understandable that you're curious," Dad said. "Anyone in your situation would be. And it's probably best that you find out the truth before your ability becomes too powerful for you to control it."

A long pause settled over the table. My parents glanced

at each other, as if trying to decide who would go next. My dad's words stuck in my mind like a splinter. *Before your ability becomes too powerful for you to control it.* What was that supposed to mean?

"The truth is," Mom said, "you're different from other kids—other *people.*"

I felt my shoulders tighten. I didn't like the way this was going.

"You're Gyfted," Dad said, and he spelled the word out for me. "*G-y-f-t-e-∂.* It stands for Genetic Youth Fluctuation, Triggering Extraordinary Development."

"What does *that* mean?" I asked.

"It means . . . ," Mom began. "Well . . . it means that you have a . . ."

"A *what?*"

Mom took a deep breath. "A superpower."

6

Learning that you have a superpower is a significant moment in the life of any Gyfted youngster. Some will be thrilled by the news. Others, not so much.

I looked across the table at my parents. "Why didn't you tell me this sooner?" I asked.

There'd been a time in my life when I'd almost expected something like this to happen. I mean, both my parents had powers, right? But whenever I'd brought it up, they'd always changed the subject. I'd started to think I wasn't like them after all, that I was a normal kid. Or maybe I'd just wished to be normal so much, I thought it would eventually come true.

"We wanted to tell you," Dad said. "We really did. But your mother and I . . . we—"

THE DREAD DUO

Plots to destroy the world, mutant
houseplants, life-threatening inventions—
these are the things you deal with
when your parents are two of the
most fearsome supervillains on earth.

"We wanted you to have a normal childhood," Mom said.

"Normal? In case you forgot, you tried to destroy the world yesterday. You call that *normal*?"

"It's true that our situation is a little . . . unconventional. Which is exactly why we wanted to wait until the right moment before telling you about your Gyft."

"You see, at this stage in development your power is referred to as a Gyft," Mom explained in her most professorial voice. "Your abilities haven't fully advanced to maturity."

"For the first ten or twelve years, a Gyfted child is just like any other child," Dad went on. "The Gyft doesn't surface until a certain stage of hormonal development."

"In other words, around your age."

"So what is it, then?" I asked.

Mom gave me a quizzical look. "What is *what*?"

"My Gyft?" The word sounded strange coming out of my mouth. "What kind of power do I have?" A whole list of possibilities scrolled through my head. Invisibility. Flight. Mind reading.

My parents looked at each other again. A long silence hung in the air around us. Finally Dad spoke. "From your description, it sounds like . . . spontaneous combustion."

I blinked. "Spontaneous combustion? You mean . . . I can make things blow up?"

"Exactly," Mom said.

"Spontaneously," Dad remarked. "Your Gyft is extremely unique. It has the capacity to be more powerful than anything we've ever seen. But it's also volatile, difficult to control."

I thought back on all the strange things that had happened to me recently. The exploding pencil. The butt-shaped burn mark. The surge of energy. This explained all of it.

"We know this is a lot to take in," Mom said. "And we have something we'd like to give you. We'd been waiting for the right occasion, and . . . well, this seems like it."

She left the room for a minute. When she came back, she was carrying a book. I glanced at the title as she handed it to me.

The Handbook for Gyfted Children.

"We thought this might be useful," Dad said.

"It's an instruction manual for kids like you," Mom added.

I opened the book and flipped through the first few chapters. I could feel my parents watching me, waiting for some kind of a response. To be honest, I didn't really know what to say. The past two days had been pretty rough. My parents had tried to destroy the world, the houseplant had threatened to kill me, and now I'd found out that I was a human microwave oven.

I'd had no idea sixth grade would be so stressful.

And I doubted a *book* was really going to make everything better.

"About this power," I said, thinking out loud, "I don't have to use it for evil, right?"

My parents looked at me like I'd just said that the moon was made out of mozzarella.

"What do you mean?" Mom asked.

"I mean . . . I wouldn't *have* to be a supervillain. I could just be an ordinary person. Who sometimes makes things explode. Spontaneously."

I could see a look of disappointment come over my parents' faces.

"What's so wrong with being a supervillain?" Dad asked. "*We're* supervillains. Your grandparents were supervillains."

"Yeah, but . . . haven't you ever thought about what would happen if—if one of your plans actually succeeded?"

Mom's eyes dropped to her plate. Dad fiddled with his silverware. I could see that the question made my parents uncomfortable, but I pressed ahead anyway.

"What if Captain Justice *hadn't* shown up yesterday?" I asked. "Were you really gonna flood the earth?"

"The government was close to meeting our demands," Dad said. "If we'd just had a little more time . . ."

His voice faded into silence. No matter how they tried to explain it, my parents knew the truth. If they actually got their way, the rest of the world would suffer.

"We realize this is hard for you, Joshua," Mom said. "But just give it some time. If you decide you want to do something else, then . . . that's your choice. We only want to help you make an educated decision."

"That's why we wanted you to have this book." Dad pointed to *The Handbook for Gyfted Children*.

"And why we were hoping you might come with us to the Vile Fair tomorrow," Mom added.

The Vile Fair was some kind of big supervillain convention that happened every year in New York City. My parents always went, but this was the first time they'd invited me along.

"I don't know," I said. "That's not really my thing."

"How do you know if you've never been?" Mom pointed out.

"Most people have a very narrow idea of what a supervillain is," Dad went on. "There's so much more to it than costumes and elaborate plans for world domination. It's a very diverse industry. And it wouldn't be right for you to dismiss a future in supervillainy without even knowing what the business is all about, right?"

"Think of it as a learning experience," Mom added.

I didn't like the sound of this. Learning experiences usually turned out to be boring experiences.

"If you really don't want to go," Mom said, "you could stay home and take care of Micus while we're gone."

On second thought, I decided the Vile Fair wouldn't be that bad.

7

You may notice your body undergoing many strange and surprising developments. You experience growth spurts, your voice changes, you begin noticing superpowers where there weren't any superpowers before. This is all part of discovering that you're Gyfted: Genetic Youth Fluctuation, Triggering Extraordinary Development.

I watched the trees and power lines blur past the window of my parents' Volvo. It was two hours from Sheepsdale to Manhattan, which gave me some time to read *The Handbook for Gyfted Children*.

A lot of the writing was pretty cheesy, and there were definitely a few chapters ("Summer Camps for Superheroes," "My Mutant and Me") that I planned to skip. But there was also a lot of helpful information. An entire chapter on how to choose whether to be a superhero or a supervillain. Tips on how to control your Gyft. Profiles of major figures in the super community, like Captain Justice, Scarlett Flame, and even my parents.

As long as I was stuck with this weird power, I figured I ought to at least know a little about what it meant and how to use it.

As we approached New York, I watched the tall buildings emerge over the horizon, glimmering in the morning sunlight. The traffic got crazier when we reached the city. I jolted forward and sideways as Dad navigated our station wagon through crowded intersections between swarms of jostling cabs. Finally the car lurched to a halt.

"Are you sure this is the right place?" I asked. A massive warehouse loomed outside my window. Its steel walls were brown with rust and covered in graffiti. The windows were shattered. The place looked like it was about to cave in on itself.

"They had to choose a location that wouldn't be too conspicuous," Mom said. "Otherwise, police and superheroes might find out about it."

Out of nowhere, a burly man in a red jacket approached the driver's window. I instinctively reached for the lock button. Then I noticed the tag on the man's jacket.

VALET
We are not responsible for lost, stolen, damaged, or irreversibly transformed items.
PLEASE REMEMBER TO TIP!

Dad rolled down his window. The valet leaned forward, a clipboard in one hand, and asked to see my dad's identification. Dad handed over his driver's license. The valet inspected his clipboard, then handed back the card.

"Welcome to the Vile Fair," he said. "Please step out of the car."

We did as we were told. Once we were out of the car, the valet reached into his jacket pocket and pulled out a small silver device. He nonchalantly pointed the device at our car and pressed a button. An explosion of sparks, a puff of smoke, and suddenly the car was nothing more than a chunk of metal, about the size of a cell phone.

The valet picked the miniature car off the ground and handed it to Dad, who slipped it into his pocket and gave the valet a couple of dollars.

"When we're ready to leave, we just give the car back to him," Dad said as we walked up the stairs toward the warehouse. "He'll zap the car again and bring it back to its previous size."

"Is that safe?" I asked.

"There are usually a few extra scratches after the resizing process. But it's better than trying to find a parking space in the city."

As we entered through the main doors, I looked around in awe. The inside of the building was nothing like the outside. I had expected a room full of rusted metal and broken bricks, but what I saw was glimmering polished steel and huge video monitors on the walls, service desks and leather sofas in the reception area.

The vast room was packed with villains. They moved around the floor in their uniforms, chatting with each other and looking into the various stands that were spread out in long rows. Above each stand was a sign with the name of the company and the product that was being displayed.

KLARGON CAPES:
FASHIONABLE AND FIRE-REPELLANT

V-LIST: THE INTERNET DATING SITE
EXCLUSIVELY FOR VILLAINS

REBECCA'S ORGANIC MUTANT FOOD: WHEN ONLY
THE BEST WILL DO FOR YOUR MUTANT

I followed my parents past a woman in an aluminum bikini and matching helmet. She was speaking to a massive bodybuilder type with concrete for skin. A group of Japanese villains appeared to be comparing their laser cannons. An elderly man zoomed past on a hover wheelchair.

In a nearby booth, a woman was demonstrating zombie obedience techniques. Mom stopped to watch.

"Throughout history," the woman said, "zombies have offered an effective means to horrify the masses. Unfortunately, working with zombies can present significant difficulties. They are nearly impossible to control, they have an insatiable appetite for brains, and they have terrible grooming habits."

She turned to face the zombie next to her. He was gray-skinned, with dark eyes and bloodstained lips. A chain held him to the edge of the booth.

"However," the woman went on, "I would like to show you that it *is* possible to train zombies so they will be aggressive, bloodthirsty heathens, but with a sense of respect for their owners' commands."

She pointed at the zombie with one outstretched finger.

"Sit," she said.

The zombie took a seat in the chair beside him.

"Now speak," she commanded.

"BLARRRGH!"

"Very good!" The woman turned to us. "Now comes the crucial part. We must reward the zombie for good behavior. Otherwise he'll have no incentive for obedience in the future. But we all know that rewarding him by feeding him brains will only send him into an uncontrollable killing frenzy."

Mom nodded.

"I believe I have found the perfect compromise," the woman said.

She reached into a cooler and removed a squishy pink

substance. The zombie leaned forward in his chair enthusiastically.

"As you can see, this has the look and texture of brains. It also smells and tastes remarkably similar. But it's actually"—she lowered her voice—"tofu."

She tossed a handful of the tofu to the zombie. He devoured it in one horrifying bite.

"This refreshing and nutritious snack will keep your zombies satisfied and obedient. And because it's not real brains, they won't go on a wild killing rampage unless you give the order."

Everyone clapped. Mom purchased three boxes.

We wandered deeper into the hall. Along the way, I saw every kind of supervillain I could imagine (and many others I couldn't). A pair of sword-wielding Siamese twins. A man whose head was composed of fire. Groups of international villains chatting with each other in languages I didn't recognize. Insane scientists. Sane scientists. Evil billionaires screaming into their cell phones. Dictators speaking with government contractors.

Every once in a while, my parents would bump into someone they knew and I would have to stand around while they chatted about some new model of utility belt they'd seen or about which supervirus was the deadliest.

At the center of the conference hall was a stage. And

in the center of the stage was a man. He was bald, with an eye patch, and a long scar down the side of his face. In his hand, he was gripping a cane with a handle that was shaped like a skull.

"That's Phineas Vex!" Dad said, pointing.

"Who?"

"The head of VexaCorp Industries."

This rang a bell. I'd seen the VexaCorp logo on all sorts of things around our house. It was the company that had manufactured my parents' hover scooters, utility belts, and plasma guns. Every season, a new VexaCorp catalog arrived in the mail. It was thicker than the phone book.

"I've been trying for years to get VexaCorp to buy one of my inventions," Dad said. "Just imagine it—supervillains across the world using something that *I* made."

I glanced back at Phineas Vex. He was standing in front of a microphone, staring across the crowd with an intense glimmer in his one good eye. On either side of him, the VexaCorp logo swirled across dozens of sky-blue flat-screen TV sets.

VEXACORP INDUSTRIES®
THE BRAND YOU TRUST AND SOCIETY FEARS

Vex leaned toward the microphone. "Greetings to my villainous brethren!" His voice boomed across the hall.

The crowd cheered. Vex waited until the cheering died away, then began to speak again.

"I, along with everyone at VexaCorp Industries, would like to welcome you to the twelfth annual Vile Fair," he said.

The entire hall burst into applause.

"A lot has changed in the supervillain community in the forty years since I started VexaCorp," Vex said. "The modern evil mastermind is no longer the two-dimensional figure from dusty old comic books. Nowadays, a villain has to view his job from a global context that integrates technology and efficiency with a capable media strategy. Together, we've made significant progress. International conflict has risen more than three hundred percent, and global villainy is at an all-time high."

Another wave of applause swept through the hall.

"But there is still plenty of room for us to improve," Vex said. "At VexaCorp, we're constantly working on new technologies that will make your life easier. Software that can simplify your schedules so that you can balance evil schemes *and* time with family. Or the newest generations of hover vehicles—cars, scooters, and SUVs—that will ensure you can go wherever you want to go, whenever you want to go there."

As Vex spoke, images drifted across the flat-screens all around him—supervillains gathered around a computer, a green-skinned woman loading groceries into the trunk of her hover SUV, children trying on their capes for the first time as their beaming parents watched.

"However, the greatest innovation can't be measured in a microchip. It can't be plugged in or tried on. It wasn't manufactured in a lab or assembled in a factory. No, the greatest innovation is much simpler than that. The greatest innovation is *you.*"

Holding the microphone in one hand and his cane in the other, Vex stepped to the front of the stage.

"*You* are the reason that superheroes lose sleep at night," he said. "*You* strike fear into the hearts of feeble humans. *You* interrupt the local news with terrifying and elaborate threats; *you* alter the weather in strange and distressing ways."

I noticed Dad nod at this last point.

"Without you," Vex said, "none of our services matter. We are here because we believe in the awful things you are doing. That's why we do our best—so you can do your worst!"

The crowd broke into raucous applause. I was surprised to find that I was clapping too. I still felt skeptical about all the evil schemes and terrible threats, but for the first time, I could actually understand what was so appealing about the lifestyle of a supervillain. It was a form of power, a way to take control in an uncontrollable world.

The cheering seemed to go on for a lot longer this time. The conference hall filled with noise. Feet stomping, shouts. Glancing behind me, I noticed that people weren't cheering at all. They were *screaming*.

Something had gone horribly wrong.

8

Getting together with others in the super community can be fun and informative!

Villains near the back of the room ran for the exits, knocking each other over, drawing their weapons. Vex had cut off his speech. The noise was overwhelming.

I looked out over the mob, and that was when I saw the smoke.

It drifted into the back of the conference hall like a dark cloud. But as it approached, I realized it wasn't *drifting* at all. It was walking.

The smoke was shaped like a human. And it moved like a human too.

It was more than six feet tall, with all the dimensions of a man. Two legs, two arms. Strands of smoke where its fingers would be. But its body was nothing more than a cloud, and its face was a dark, formless haze.

Phineas Vex was standing on the stage, watching the smoke creature with a mixture of confusion and fear. VexaCorp employees surrounded him. He tried to speak into the microphone, but his voice was overwhelmed by the screams that filled the space.

A VexaCorp security guard jumped down from the stage, firing a plasma cannon, but the beam passed right through the creature. It was like trying to shoot a cloud. Before the security guard could fire off another round, the creature stretched out its smoky hand and took hold of the man's neck. Instantly the guard dropped his plasma cannon. The man struggled to kick the thing, but his elbows and feet passed harmlessly through the dark smoke.

The creature gripped the man tighter, surrounding him in a dark cloud that pitched and swirled like a tornado. A burst of lightning shot through the darkness. And just like that, the security guard was gone.

A wave of horror passed over me as I saw that there were more of the smoke creatures. They were everywhere. There must've been twenty, maybe thirty, of them, each shaped like a human, and each indestructible in every way. They stalked across the room, taking hold of anyone in their path. As soon as they had someone in their grip, it was always the same—

A dark swirl of clouds.

A burst of lightning.

And then the person vanished. Gone.

"Wh-what are those things?" I asked.

Dad looked down at me. His face was as pale as ice. "I don't know," he said. "I've never seen anything like them before."

The inside of the conference hall was a madhouse. Screams filled the air. People knocked into each other. Villains on hover scooters flew near the ceiling, looking down at the terrible scene. Others blasted holes in the wall to get away. Some tried using their powers against the smoke monsters. Fireballs, freeze rays, sonic booms. But nothing worked.

A shiver of fear ran down my neck. If these things couldn't be stopped by a huge building full of super-villains, then the rest of the world didn't stand a chance.

I was knocked to the ground by a mob of people running toward an exit. I turned in time to see what the group was running from.

One of the smoke creatures was heading toward me.

Its featureless face turned in my direction. As I tried to stagger away, my feet slipped on a pile of Cheswick's Vintage Villain Uniforms and I fell to the floor again.

The creature was only a few feet away. Its arm reached out.

I rolled under the table of vintage uniforms and out the other side just as the thing grabbed for my leg. Clambering to my feet, I began to run. Pushing through a screaming crowd, I managed to lose the smoke creature in the maze of smoldering booths. To my left, I caught sight of the stage. Vex looked like he was trying to climb down to the floor level, as if he wanted to personally fight the smoke creatures who'd interrupted his speech, but a team of bodyguards held him back.

Next to the stage, I spotted my parents huddled behind an overturned speaker. Dad was desperately looking out over the madness. Mom called out for me. And from where I was standing, I could see something they couldn't. A smoke creature was approaching them from behind.

I tried screaming their names, but my voice was swallowed by all the other sounds in the hall. From this distance, there was no way to get their attention. Panic clutched my heart. Behind my parents, the smoke creature stalked closer. It would reach them any second.

Without another thought, I took off running as fast as I could—straight for the smoke creature. I knew it was a crazy thing to do. I should've been running away from them—*not* toward them. But my parents were in danger.

SMOKE CREATURE!

An unstoppable monster that's over six
feet tall, made of smoke, and capable
of terrorizing even the deadliest
supervillains. Unless you want
to vanish in a bolt of lightning,
this guy is not to be messed with.

I couldn't just stand by and watch them vanish in a flash of lightning.

My feet pounded the floor. Halfway there, I passed by the zombie obedience booth we'd visited earlier. Now the trainer was gone. And so was the zombie. Its chain hung broken next to a pile of uneaten tofu.

Without slowing down, I grabbed a handful of the tofu and threw it as hard as I could at the smoke creature. I'm not sure what I expected to happen. If all the devious gadgetry and special powers in the hall hadn't been able to harm the creatures, I doubted a blob of meat substitute would do the trick. But as the tofu left my hand, it wasn't pink any longer. It was as black as a piece of charcoal. Fire trailed it through the air as though it were a missile.

Spontaneous combustion. It had somehow allowed me to transform a lump of tofu into a fiery projectile rocket.

Like all the other weaponry in the convention hall, the charred tofu brains sailed right through the creature. But at least I'd managed to get the thing's attention. It stopped moving toward my parents and turned its dark, cloudy head toward me. Then it began walking my way.

"Joshua!" Dad called. "Get out of there!"

I turned to run, but that was as far as I got. Behind me was another smoke creature. I was surrounded.

My options had dwindled away to nothing. The creatures stalked toward me from both sides. Flaming booths blocked any chance of escape. And I didn't even have any tofu left.

I could hear my parents calling out to me, but there was nothing either of them could do. It was too late. The smoke creatures were closing in. The one closest to me reached out. Its cloudy fingers were circling my neck when I heard another voice.

"Stop right there!"

The voice was deep, authoritative—both familiar and unfamiliar at the same time. The smoke creature and I both turned to look at the man who had just spoken.

It was Phineas Vex. Up close, he looked different somehow. The scar stood out, like a ribbon running down his bald scalp. His eye patch glimmered from the lights overhead. His other eye—the good one—shifted until it found me. He focused on me, the eye narrowing as he spoke.

"Run!" Although his voice was quiet, the word seemed to vibrate in my chest. "Get out of here! Now!"

Vex raised his cane above his head and swung it at the smoke creature. I didn't see what happened next. I was already running toward my parents.

Mom and Dad took me in their arms.

"I'm so glad you're safe," Mom whispered into my ear.

"What about Vex!" I twisted to look behind me. What I saw sent a shiver through my entire body.

Vex was now in the smoke creature's grip, hanging a

foot above the ground. His legs swung limply beneath him like an oversized rag doll's. His cane dropped to the ground.

"We can't just leave him!" I screamed, trying to free myself from my parents' arms.

The more I struggled, the more they pulled me back. I looked around, seeking something—anything—I could throw at the thing. But it was already too late. The smoke had Vex surrounded, a chaotic mass of twisting darkness. In the next moment, the cloud filled with a blast of lightning.

And then Vex was gone.

"We have to get out of here." Mom's voice was quiet and firm. "Now."

I felt myself being pulled. With my parents on either side of me, we staggered over the demolished ruins of disintegrated booths.

Halfway to the exit, Dad came to a sudden halt. The shift in momentum nearly sent me tumbling to the ground. He reached one gloved hand into a pile of wreckage, and whatever it was he found, he carefully slipped it into a pouch connected to his utility belt before I could get a look.

Then we were moving again, running through the burning convention hall toward the exits.

9

Don't believe everything you read.

At school the rumors about Sophie Smith had only gotten crazier over the weekend. Now the Cafeteria Girls were saying that she was a recluse with obsessive-compulsive disorder.

"That's why she doesn't have any friends," said one of them.

I thought about pointing out that maybe Sophie might not have any friends because she'd been at Sheepsdale Middle School for only a total of one and a half days, but kept my mouth shut because (a) the Cafeteria Girls didn't actually know that I existed, and (b) I was worried what kind of things they'd say about me if they ever found out that I *did* exist.

"Not to mention her dad's a complete psycho," one of the girls said. "I heard there's a room in his house that's filled with torture devices."

The entire table gasped.

"Seriously?"

"Seriously. There are, like, all these high-tech machines with sharp points and crazy-looking straps. Really painful-looking stuff."

"But . . . why would he need torture devices?"

"Because he tortures people. Duh!"

The girls went silent at the thought of this. It was without a doubt the longest period of silence in the history of the Cafeteria Girls, and it was only interrupted when the bell rang.

"Can you believe that?" Milton said once we'd left the cafeteria. "Sophie's dad must be insane!"

I stopped walking outside the doorway to the debate hall and looked back at Milton.

"Have you ever thought that some of the stuff we hear about people at this school is made up?" I asked.

"What do you mean?"

"I mean, those girls aren't always reliable."

"Maybe, but . . ." Milton unzipped his backpack and reached inside. "Wait till you see *this*."

Milton pulled out a magazine. The title stretched across the top section of the cover:

SUPER SCOOP

I'd seen it in supermarkets, always full of gossip about celebrity superheroes and supervillains. According to my parents, *Super Scoop* was a trashy tabloid that made the Cafeteria Girls look like a professional fact-checking department. Maybe that was why it was so popular.

On the cover of this week's issue was a photograph of Captain Justice. Beside the photo was a block of bold text:

CAPTAIN CAUGHT CANOODLING!

Captain Justice was standing next to a tall, slender woman with fiery red hair and a matching cape. She was wearing sunglasses and holding a coffee cup. They looked to be frozen in a moment of laughter at something one of them had just said, obviously unaware that they were being photographed.

"That's Scarlett Flame!" Milton said, pointing at the red-haired woman. "She's the one who fought the Abominator on the roof of the Empire State Building. There's tons of cool stuff in here!"

My mom had a different opinion about *Super Scoop*. "Trashy magazines like that give us all a bad reputation," she had whispered to me the last time we'd passed an issue in the checkout line at the grocery store. I'd wanted to point out that trying to destroy the world probably didn't do much for their rep either.

Mom had probably still been upset about the cover story from a few months earlier entitled, "The Botanist: Is She Getting TOO Close to Her Zombies?" This had been accompanied by a photo of Mom supposedly kissing one of her zombies. Actually, the zombie had been trying to bite her ear off, but the magazine hadn't mentioned that.

"It's not even real journalism," Mom had complained. "It's just *lies*. Who buys this junk?"

"My mom subscribes," Milton said now, grinning. "I always look through the new issues when they show up at our house."

He flipped excitedly through the magazine's pages.

"Here's an article about this Mexican supervillain, El Diablo Gigantico, who's supposedly trying to make it big in America now. And this kid nFinity—he's only fifteen, but he's already one of the most famous superheroes in the country. Oh, and this article about the Dread Duo . . ."

Milton pointed to an extremely unflattering photo of my parents. The title of the article was stamped across half the glossy page in massive letters:

The Dread Duo—Fiends or Frauds?

"Remember Dr. Dread from the other day?" Milton asked, nodding at the shadowy image of my dad.

"He was that guy who tried to flood the earth, right?" I said, like I wasn't entirely sure.

"It says here that he's not even a real doctor. He just added 'Dr.' to his name because it sounds more sinister."

"That's not true! He got his PhD in engineering at—" I stopped when I noticed the confused expression on Milton's face.

"I thought you didn't pay any attention to this stuff," he said.

"I don't. I just meant that— Er . . . I read that he *is* a real doctor. On the Internet. But then again, maybe he's not."

Milton stared at me for a second longer, then shrugged, glancing back at the magazine. He paged through a few more articles. Glossy photos of superheroes and super-villains walking their dogs, jogging with mutants, waving at fans. I caught my breath when I noticed the next headline.

Violence at the Vile Fair!

Underneath was a grainy photograph of one of the smoke creatures. Just looking at it sent a spasm of fear through my body. But before I could read anything else, Milton had flipped forward to the next article.

"This is what I wanted to show you!" He pointed to

the page. "It says that there was a big shipment of robot parts to a house in Sheepsdale. Do you have any idea what someone would need robot parts for?"

I shook my head.

"Robots! That's what!"

Milton checked over his shoulder, then turned back to me.

"I wonder if this has something to do with Sophie's dad," he whispered. "It doesn't say where in Sheepsdale, or who, but . . . *what if it's him?* I mean, it's just like what the Cafeteria Girls were talking about, with all the torture devices and machine guns and stuff. Whoever her dad is, he's gotta be into some crazy stuff. I'll bet he ordered the robot parts too."

"Maybe . . ." My brain was still stuck on the earlier page about the Vile Fair. "Hey, can I borrow that magazine?"

Milton's eyes narrowed. "I thought you didn't like *Super Scoop*."

"I just wanted to find out more about the . . . er—"

"Robot parts?"

"Exactly."

Milton's face broke into a grin. "See? I told you it's interesting." Closing the magazine, he pushed it into my hand.

I said goodbye to Milton and hurried to my locker, where I opened *Super Scoop* to the Vile Fair article. In the time since we'd gotten back from New York, I hadn't been able to stop thinking about what had happened.

But after reading the article twice, I was still clueless. Nobody knew what the smoke creatures were or who was behind the attack. The super community was teeming with speculation—that the smoke creatures had been sent by a superhero, or a villain looking to cut into the competition, or even a business rival of Phineas Vex. The only thing everyone could agree on was that they were all afraid of what would happen next.

Nobody felt safe.

"Hey, Joshua."

The voice made me flinch. Shoving the magazine into my backpack, I whirled around. Sophie Smith was standing behind me.

"I just wanted to check if you've started thinking about topics for our project yet," she said.

"Oh . . ." *The history project.* With everything else that had been going on (finding out I had a superpower, getting chased around a convention hall by smoke creatures—you know, that kind of thing), it had completely slipped my mind. "I've been sort of busy."

"Same here." Sophie smiled, like she was relieved she wasn't the only one. "I'm still trying to find my way to all my classes."

"I could show you around if you want."

The words were out there before I'd even realized

what I'd said. Here I was talking with a girl whose dad possibly kept torture devices lying around the house, and I was offering to give her an orientation tour?

My voice rose as I tried to explain myself. "What I mean is, I moved a lot too when I was younger. So I know that it can make you feel like a freak."

Sophie's smile faded.

"Not that I think you're a freak!" I added quickly. "You're very non-freaky, believe me. I was just—"

"It's okay," Sophie said. "I know what you mean. Every time I show up in a new town, I think, *This is going to be the place where we finally end up.* But it never is. Sometimes I just feel like . . . like luggage. As soon as I meet a few people, my dad says we have to pack up and move again."

Now that she'd mentioned her dad, I was halfway tempted to ask about him. I thought about the crazy rumors swirling around Sophie's home life. And the way she'd introduced herself in class the other day, like she was still getting used to saying her name out loud.

But Sophie was already backpedaling away from me. "Better get going," she said quickly. "See you in seventh period."

She disappeared into the crowded hallway before I had a chance to say goodbye.

10

Make time to practice your Gyft.

Ever since returning from the Vile Fair on Saturday, my parents had been working nearly non-stop in their lab. It was no different when I got home that afternoon. I heard the quiet *whoosh* of a Bunsen burner upstairs, and the murmur of muffled voices.

Settling onto the couch, I opened *The Handbook for Gyfted Children* to the chapter titled "Practicing Your Powers." There was a lot of technical advice relating to specific powers. For example, if you had the Gyft of flight, it was a bad idea to practice under a ceiling fan. But the basic idea of the chapter was pretty simple. If you wanted your Gyft to work, you needed to do three things:

Practice a lot

Control your emotions

Focus your mind

I searched the house for something to practice on, until I found the ceramic lawn gnome that had been sitting in a box ever since Aunt Linda had given it to my mom years before. The gnome had bright cheeks, a pointed hat, and a weird-looking smile. I figured my mom wouldn't mind if it exploded.

I took the gnome up to my bedroom and sat down next to it on the floor, concentrating on its long beard and its funny grin. I held out my hands, thinking about sparks raining down from my fingertips, trying to imagine the gnome's little pointed hat combusting. I reached down and gripped the lawn gnome around its chubby ceramic belly . . .

And nothing happened. The gnome looked just as it had before. Same pointed hat. Same goofy grin. Not even a burn mark.

I closed my eyes and tried to block out all my distractions. But I couldn't get Sophie out of my mind. It was as if the more I tried to forget her, the more I thought about her. I opened my eyes. The gnome's expression was starting to look kind of smug, like he knew I would fail.

Gritting my teeth with frustration, I pushed the gnome aside and slammed my fists down onto the carpet.

BOOM!

It sounded like a firecracker had gone off. In the next instant, the carpet erupted into flames.

I fell backward as the fire spread. Smoke billowed up to the ceiling. Scrambling to my feet, I tripped over my chair and staggered into the hallway. I grabbed a fire extinguisher from the closet and charged back into my room.

Behind me, I could hear my parents' footsteps pounding the floorboards. The smoke alarm was wailing.

Shielding my face with one hand, I lifted the fire extinguisher and pointed the hose.

White liquid shot out of the end of the nozzle, smothering the flames. Seconds later, my parents appeared in my doorway, their faces pale.

"What *happened*?" Mom asked.

My carpet was black and charred. Half my bedspread was ruined. White fire extinguisher goo was everywhere.

"Just practicing," I said.

Over the next two weeks, I spent every spare moment training. In the mornings, I concentrated on heating up my toast. In PE, I tested my power out on my gym shorts (*not* while I was wearing them). After school, I went onto the back porch (bringing the fire extinguisher with me, just in case) to try out my spontaneous combustion on twigs, leaves, and clumps of dried grass.

I brought *The Handbook for Gyfted Children* to school with me sometimes, hiding it between the covers of my books and reading whenever I could. When I came across a part that seemed useful, I wrote it down in my notebook. Even though I wasn't sure how all these notes were supposed to help me in the end, I kept writing them down. Doing it made me feel a little better, like I wasn't alone.

Soon I could set fire to leaves and cause sticks to explode. Of course, this was small stuff. I still hadn't tested my Gyft on anything bigger than a lawn gnome.

At least not until I got a chance to try it out on Joey and Brick.

I got to school a little earlier than usual on Thursday. I'd been so busy practicing over the past weeks that I'd pretty much ignored everything else, including school. I was hoping to catch up on some homework before first period. Instead, I ran into Joey and Brick.

They were waiting for me at my locker. It seemed strange that they were there so early. I guess for them, bullying was an extracurricular activity.

"Hey, Dorkface," Joey said. "We've been looking for you."

The rest of the hallway was empty. Brick began to walk in my direction, Joey following close behind.

"We know all about you," Joey said. "You're some kind of freak. You should be in a circus, not in a school."

My first instinct was to run. My second and third instincts were pretty much the same. I could already imagine the consequences of sticking around. Teasing, pushing, punching, locker-stuffing, swirlies, noogies, wedgies, nedgies.

But I had something they didn't. Spontaneous combustion.

Just a jolt, that was all it would take. Maybe a little fireball, for dramatic effect. Nothing too big. I didn't want to have to explain to Principal Sloane why two students had exploded before first period.

"How'd it happen?" Joey asked, getting closer. "Didja wake up one morning knowing you were a freak? Or maybe you got bit by a radioactive worm."

Brick let out a laugh. He was getting really close now.

I thought about electric fences, spark plugs, malfunctioning toasters.

They were five feet away.

Three feet.

I held out my arms, flexing my muscles and concentrating my energy. I took a deep breath, summoned all my power, and . . .

Brick threw me into the girls' bathroom.

The door flew open, and I landed with a thud on the hard tile floor. Fortunately, the restroom was empty. I staggered to my feet. There'd been no shock, no jolt. There hadn't even been a spark. What kind of a lousy superpower *was* this? All that practice, and when I needed it most—nothing.

My parents had said my power would be difficult to control. I guess that was why they called it *spontaneous* combustion.

Through the door, I could hear Joey and Brick out in the hallway. They were trying to intimidate me. Screaming. Banging on lockers. Throwing things around.

To be honest, it sounded like overkill to me. They had already tossed me into the girls' bathroom. Why not just punch me in the stomach, hang me by my underwear from the basketball hoop, and get it over with already?

I curled my hands into fists, waiting. But the door stayed closed.

All of a sudden, the noises stopped. No more clanging, no more screaming. Just silence.

Opening the door, I glanced into the hallway. What I saw was beyond anything I could've ever imagined.

11

Because only a small fraction of the population is born with a superpower, the chances of meeting another Gyfted child are tiny.

Several lockers had been ripped apart, leaving gaping holes where the doors had been. Books and papers were strewn everywhere. Joey and Brick were lying on the floor, moaning in pain. Four locker doors were curled around them. They were trapped up to their necks inside the twisted sheets of steel, like human burritos.

The screams I'd heard had been screams of *pain*.

Joey and Brick were in shock, staring blankly into space, mumbling to themselves. I almost felt sorry for them. Almost.

I crouched down next to Joey. "Who did this to you?"

I asked. My parents couldn't have been responsible. They might have been supervillains, but they still had boundaries.

"Never seen anything like it . . . ," Joey muttered. "Didn't look human."

"Who? Who're you talking about?"

Joey's only response was a whimper.

Behind me, I heard the steady click of footsteps. Spinning around, I glimpsed a girl walking quickly in the other direction.

It was impossible to be sure, but I could've sworn it was Sophie Smith.

A middle school is not a good place to keep a secret. News of what happened to Joey and Brick passed through Sheepsdale Middle School like wildfire.

The story changed each time I heard it. The basic information was all there—the bent locker doors, the books and papers spilled across the hall—but other details had been added along the way. By the time seventh period came around, it was out of control.

"They were hanging upside down with their underwear on their heads!" Milton said.

He was barely able to contain his excitement. We were in our usual desks, near the back of the room.

"Every single locker in the hallway had been ripped to shreds," Milton went on. "And there was fire too! Lots of fire! You wanna know the best part?"

"What?" I said, trying not to sound too doubtful.

"Joey was crying out for his mama!" Milton burst into laughter.

Everyone was thrilled to see the two biggest bullies in the school get beaten up and humiliated. But no matter how much I hated them, I couldn't share in this excitement. I needed to know who had done this.

And apparently, I wasn't the only one.

"Who do *you* think did it?" Milton asked Sophie as soon as she got to class.

She shifted in her seat. "I don't know. Probably just a freak accident."

"No way! It had to be someone in this school. And I wanna find out *who*!"

"Anyway," Sophie said, sounding like she wanted to change the subject. "When do you guys want to work on our project? Our presentation's next week. I was thinking we could meet up tomorrow."

"Hey, why don't we go to the Chilled Grease Diner?" Milton said. "It'll be fun!"

The Chilled Grease Diner was this place a few blocks from school. It was kind of a dump. But it also served all-you-can-eat curly fries, which meant that it was Milton's favorite restaurant.

"Wasn't that the place where some guy found a thumb in his omelet?" Sophie asked.

"Only the *tip*," Milton explained. "And it wasn't a big deal. They didn't even charge the guy for the omelet, so I don't know why he was complaining."

Sophie shrugged. "Sounds good. What about you, Joshua?"

Her voice sounded like it was coming from the end of a tunnel. All my attention was trained on something else. Something I'd just noticed. A jagged rip ran halfway down Sophie's sleeve. It looked as if her shirt had been snagged by a nail. Or a large sheet of metal.

Suddenly it all added up. The glimpse of her in the hallway this morning. The ripped sleeve. *She* was the one who'd beaten up Joey and Brick. But how? The only people who could create that kind of destruction were people like my parents or Captain Justice. People with superpowers. Did that mean that Sophie was . . .

Gyfted?

Curiosity flared across my thoughts. Was it really possible? And if so, what kind of power did she have?

I spent all of seventh period wondering whether I should talk to her about it. If there *was* another Gyfted kid at school, I wanted to know. On the other hand, after seeing the way she'd beaten the school's biggest bullies to a pulp, I wasn't sure it was the best idea to confront her with personal questions.

As it turned out, I didn't have to decide. Because when class let out, Sophie wanted to talk to *me*.

"Hey, Joshua. Wait up."

As soon as she joined me in the crowded hallway, I had a feeling about what was coming next. Sophie was going to confess that she had a Gyft. And ask me not to tell anyone about how she went around beating up bullies and causing some serious damage to school property.

But that wasn't what she said. Instead, Sophie took a step toward me until I was looking right into her blue-gray eyes.

"I know about your Gyft," she said.

The ground dropped out from underneath me, pulling the sounds of the hallway with it. This wasn't the way it was supposed to go. I was supposed to know about *her* Gyft. Not the other way around.

"How—how did you find out?"

"I saw you reading *The Handbook for Gyfted Children* during class." She hesitated. "I . . . I have the same book."

I clenched my teeth. At the end of the hallway, I noticed Joey and Brick walking toward us. Joey had a sling around one arm. Brick had a fairly noticeable bump on his forehead. When the two of them saw Sophie, they became pale as ghosts. Joey turned and hobbled in the other direction, and Brick followed closely behind.

"Maybe we should go someplace more private," Sophie said.

We walked in silence through the exits and out past the line of waiting buses until we reached a hill that overlooked the football field.

"How long have you known that you're Gyfted?" Sophie asked.

I hesitated. It felt strange to be having this conversation with a classmate, but there wasn't any point denying it now. "Couple of weeks. What about you?"

"About a year. Girls tend to develop their Gyfts a little earlier than guys."

"And you're able to control it?"

"Kind of. At the beginning, I was clueless." Sophie gazed out across the football field. "The first time it happened, I was at soccer practice. I accidentally kicked the ball at my coach's minivan."

"So that's your power? Bad aim?"

I had to fight back the urge to laugh, but Sophie never even cracked a smile.

"When the ball slammed into it, the minivan flipped over," she said. "Then a few weeks later, during my piano lesson, I hit the keys a little too hard and the entire piano collapsed."

My eyes widened. It seemed impossible that someone as little as Sophie could leave behind such a trail of devastation.

"Superhuman strength," she said. "That's my Gyft."

Compared with superhuman strength, my power suddenly seemed a lot less impressive. I thought of all the things she was capable of—knocking over cars, beating up the school's biggest bullies. I couldn't do anything nearly that cool. I was just an oversized electrical socket.

"It's not as great as it sounds," Sophie said. "There's a side effect."

"What do you mean?"

By the way Sophie's eyes dropped to the ground, I could tell she didn't want to say any more about it. My memory flipped back to this morning. Joey lying on the hallway floor, mumbling. *Never seen anything like it,* he'd said. *Didn't look human.*

"What about you?" Sophie asked. "What's your Gyft?"

"Spontaneous combustion," I admitted. "Basically, I make stuff blow up."

I told her about the explosions, the burn marks, the weeks of practice.

"Have you met any other kids like us?" I asked her. "Kids with—superpowers?"

She shook her head. "Not many. Most Gyfted kids are too scared to talk about it. But I've met a few through friends of my dad. He, uh, grew up Gyfted too."

"Your dad?"

Sophie sighed, digging her heel into a patch of grass. "So, what have you heard about him?"

As the new kid, Sophie's a mystery
around school. But when Joshua discovers
the secret she's been hiding, he's not sure
whether they're destined to be friends...
or enemies.

"Nothing."

The look she gave me told me she could see right through my lie.

"All right. Maybe I've heard a few things," I said.

"Like what?"

I didn't really want to, but I told her everything I'd heard. The truckloads of empty boxes and countless TVs, the machine guns, the torture devices . . .

I'd expected her to deny it all, or laugh at how crazy gossip could get. Instead, she shrugged. "Yep, that sounds about right."

"Whoa. So you mean—all that stuff is true?"

Sophie nodded. "Pretty much. Except the part about torture devices. I don't think he has any of those."

"You don't *think*?"

It seemed like the kind of thing you would know for sure. Either you had torture devices or you *didn't*. But there was plenty going on in my own house that I wasn't aware of. I hadn't known about my parents' whole flooding-the-entire-world-and-blackmailing-the-government thing until the day they'd done it.

"My dad has trouble keeping his identity a secret," Sophie said. "It's part of the reason we have to move around all the time. He just enjoys the fame too much. It's always the same. People start to find out little things about him here and there. Then more of the truth comes out. And then, just like that—we pick up and move to a new town, a new school, a new fake name."

I nearly said *I know how it feels,* but I held my tongue.

"With my dad, the truth always comes out sooner or later," Sophie said. "And he just expects me to keep silent about it everywhere we go. Sometimes I get so sick of lying to everyone, you know?"

"So if your name isn't Sophie Smith," I said, "then who *are* you?"

"Promise not to tell anyone else?"

I nodded. "I'm pretty good at keeping secrets," I said. *I've done it for my parents all my life.*

Sophie glanced once more across the vacant hillside around us. "My dad is Captain Justice."

12

**For many Gyfted children,
life is full of unexpected surprises.**

Take it from me, it's not easy to find out that your project partner is the daughter of your parents' archenemy. I stared at Sophie, my mind spinning back over the past two weeks. That was how Captain Justice had gotten there so quickly when my parents had tried to flood the earth. Because he now lived in the same zip code.

"Is everything okay?" Sophie's voice cut through the silence. "You look a little freaked out."

Maybe that's because your dad tried to crush my dad underneath Mr. Chow's Chinese Buffet! I thought.

But all I said was "I've got to go."

"Why? What's wrong?"

"Nothing." I took a step backward. "I just remembered I need to be . . . somewhere else."

I spun around before she could say anything, and jogged quickly down the hill. Sophie called after me, but I didn't look back.

When I got home, my parents were still in their lab. I dropped my backpack in the living room and headed into the kitchen for a snack. Micus heaved a clump of soil at me, but I was still so caught up thinking about what Sophie had just told me that I didn't care.

How was I supposed to go to school with Captain Justice's daughter? How was I supposed to sit next to her in seventh period?

Of all the places to live, her dad had chosen Sheepsdale. The coincidence was too big to ignore. What if Captain Justice had tracked the Dread Duo here? What if he was closing in on my parents?

In the kitchen, I tried to use my Gyft on a Pop-Tart, but my mind refused to focus. The Pop-Tart remained frozen in my hands until I gave up and dropped it into the toaster.

Apparently, I wasn't the only one in the house with a lot weighing on my mind. As soon as my mom entered the kitchen, I could see the exhaustion on her face. Dark rings circled her eyes. One collar of her lab coat was stained with some kind of blue liquid.

"How're things going?" she asked, shuffling through a drawer.

"Okay. I guess."

"And how was your day at"—she paused, pushing one drawer closed and opening another—"your day at— uh . . ."

"School?" I suggested.

"Exactly. School. How was your day at school?"

"Not great. A couple of guys threw me into the girls' bathroom—"

"That's marvelous, sweetheart!" she said in the too-loud voice of someone whose mind was a hundred miles away. "You haven't seen a pair of pliers around here, have you?"

"No," I said, without making any effort to hide the annoyance in my voice. "So what are you working on?"

Mom hesitated. "Oh . . . the usual. Tinkering. Experimenting. Theorizing."

She was hiding something from me. That much was obvious. But what?

"Ah, there you are, Emily," Dad said, walking in. "Did you find those pliers?"

"Not yet, honey."

"Hmm. Maybe they're in the garage. I'll go ch—" Dad noticed me. "Oh, didn't see you there, buddy."

"I've been standing here the entire time," I said.

"Right. Of course." Dad ran a hand through his tousled hair. It looked like he hadn't shaved in a week.

"What's going on with you guys?" I asked.

Dad stared blankly into space. "What do you mean?"

"You've been spending all your time in your lab. When you *do* come out, you don't pay any attention to what's going on. Nobody's cooked or cleaned or gone shopping in days."

Mom started to speak, but then shook her head. Dad's eyes fell to the ground.

"What?" I said. "What's going on?"

My parents exchanged a long look. When Dad turned back to me, he said, "Maybe it's better if you come up to the lab with us. We have something to show you."

They led me up the stairs with heavy footsteps and slouched shoulders. Dad cast a weary-eyed glance back at me, then pushed open the lab door.

My last visit to the lab had been six months before, and that hadn't gone so well. One of my mom's zombies had mistaken me for its afternoon snack, and I'd barely made it out alive. Ever since, I'd avoided the lab entirely.

Fortunately, Mom had moved the zombies down to the basement a few months back. There were a few suspicious-looking houseplants growing under a sunlamp in one corner, but they didn't seem to have the

99

same grudge against me that Micus did. At least, not yet.

The lab always seemed to be in a state of well-organized chaos. To my left was a bookshelf, stacked with instruction manuals, textbooks on particle physics and biology, sealed glass jars containing toxic chemicals, VexaCorp catalogs. A pair of my dad's old goggles acted as a bookend. A steel table stretched across the center of the room. Its surface was scattered with glass test tubes half full of green and blue liquid. Against the wall to my right was a chalkboard, covered with obscure markings and dense equations.

I followed my parents past all this toward a glass case that was perched on top of a drafting table at the far end of the room.

"You might want to stand back," Dad said as he peered through the glass.

I wasn't sure what I had to worry about. The case was about the size of a shoe box and looked empty. But I didn't want to take any chances. I'd spent enough time around my parents to know that just because you couldn't see something didn't mean it couldn't hurt you.

I stepped away from the case. "Is this far enough?"

Dad looked back at me. "Probably."

Just to be safe, I took another step backward.

Dad opened the top drawer of a filing cabinet, reached

inside, and removed a small black device that fit into the palm of his hand.

"I invented this little gadget here to render a magnified image of objects far too small to be seen with average eyesight," he said.

"This way your father can show me the things that normally only he can see," Mom added.

"So it's a microscope?"

"It's *much* more than a microscope," Dad said, sounding a little defensive. "This device allows the user to create a 3-D image of the magnified object and then analyze it from every conceivable angle. *And* you can fit it into your pocket!"

"Your father is hoping VexaCorp will buy the design from him," Mom told me.

"The Dreadoscope," he said, staring into space as if imagining the name on a sign. "That's what I'm planning to call it. But there's no telling what will happen now that Phineas Vex is gone."

The memory caused the color to drain from Dad's face. He went silent for a moment before turning back to the glass case. Flipping a switch on the drafting table caused the top of the case to slide open. Leaning forward, Dad peered inside. He lowered the Dreadoscope into the case, carefully bringing it to rest on the bottom. When he pressed a small button on the left side of the device, an image appeared on the monitor. It looked like a silver egg with a nozzle jutting out of the front end.

"You mean to tell me that *this* is inside that glass box?"

"Exactly," Mom said. "Except on a much smaller scale."

Suddenly I realized why my dad had warned me to stand away from the glass case. It wasn't for my own safety. It was for the safety of what was inside.

"What is it?"

"Remember the smoke creatures?" Dad asked.

"You mean those unstoppable monsters that attacked a convention hall full of supervillains? No, I'd completely forgotten."

Ignoring my sarcasm, Dad pointed to the image on the monitor. "*This* is a very tiny part of the smoke creature."

"But—how?"

"The creature isn't made of smoke at all," Dad said. "It's actually a dense anthropomorphic composite of remote-programmed nano-beings."

"Oh, that clears it up." I rolled my eyes.

"What your father's trying to say," Mom explained, "is that the smoke creatures are formed by millions of tiny flying robots. Just like this one here." She nodded toward the silver egg. "Each of these robots is microscopic. Much too small to be seen by the human eye. That's why we can only observe it with a micro—"

Dad gave her a sharp look.

"I mean, *Dreadoscope*," Mom said. "If we zoom in a little, you'll see that there's something printed here."

She pointed to a spot on the robot's side. It didn't look like anything more than a smudge, but when Mom clicked the zoom button, I saw that it was something else. A logo.

Z

Walking Smoke™

"What does the *Z* stand for?" I asked.

"We don't know," Dad said. "But whoever designed this must have an unbelievable amount of money and resources in order to create such sophisticated technology."

"They were able to manufacture millions of these things," Mom said, glancing at the image of the robot. "And when they group together, they create a kind of—"

"Swarm," Dad said, shivering. "Like insects, they swarm together—so close to one another that it creates the illusion of one being. A cloud, in this case. Programmed to look and move like a human."

"We're talking about nanotechnology on a scale that nobody's ever seen before," Mom said.

"And what happens when the cloud—er, the nanobeings . . . when *it* eats someone?" I glanced nervously from my mom to my dad. "Does that person die?"

"Not as far as we can tell," Dad said. "When the nano-beings group around a person, they lose their humanlike shape. They create a portal. First they surround their victim. Then each of them fires off a concentrated energy beam from the nozzle on the front end."

"Each of these beams is far too small to be seen by the naked eye," Mom continued. "But when they're all focused on the same object, working at the same time, it looks like—"

"Lightning," I said under my breath.

A memory flickered through my mind. Phineas Vex, surrounded by the smoke, absorbed by a dark cloud. A burst of light had filled the dark space. Like lightning.

And then he was gone.

"Each energy beam is able to break apart and transport a single molecule," Mom said. "Millions of these nano-beings means millions of energy beams. The person in the center of all this is broken apart into distinct molecules, then transported, piece by piece, somewhere else. And then these molecules are reassembled in a new place. In other words, the person is teleported."

"So how did you get this thing?" I pointed to the image of the nano-being on the computer.

"Actually, we have *you* to thank for that." Dad smiled at me.

"Me? How?"

"You remember throwing that charred piece of tofu at the smoke creature?"

I nodded. That wasn't the kind of thing you forgot easily.

"Well, after the tofu spontaneously combusted, it still maintained some of its characteristic sticky texture. When you launched it at the smoke creature, a few of the nano-beings got stuck in the lump of burned tofu."

"As we were escaping from the convention hall, your father noticed the tofu—*and* what was embedded in it," Mom explained.

I remembered the chaos of the convention hall. Burning booths, rampaging smoke creatures. And the way Dad had suddenly stopped to pluck something out of the wreckage. With his superpowered eyesight, he'd spotted the nano-beings stuck in the tofu.

"When we got back home, your father and I deactivated one of the nano-beings and put it into this box to study it," Mom said. "Inside its circuitry, there's a chip programmed with the tracking coordinates. If we could access that chip, we could trace where all the villains have been transported."

I felt a glimmer of hope. "Then you could find who's doing this!"

Dad sighed. "Unfortunately, it's not that simple. Whoever designed this really knew what they were doing.

The chip is lodged in a protective titanium casing. In order to access the chip, you have to break the casing. But if you break the casing, you'll destroy the chip."

"So that's it, then? There's nothing you can do to stop these things?" The smoke creatures were still out there. They could attack again at any time.

I stared into the glass box. It looked empty, but it could destroy my family.

Mom's voice shattered the silence. "There is *one* way we might be able to access the chip," she said. "A chemical compound known as zenoplyric acid. It's extremely dangerous."

"We tried to steal a cargo of it two years ago, but Captain Justice had to get in the way." Dad glared angrily at the drafting table. "He nearly broke my ankle that time, the big jerk."

"*Anyway,*" Mom went on, "a small amount of zenoplyric acid could dissolve the titanium casing around the chip—"

"Without destroying the chip itself—"

"Allowing us to track where the supervillains are being transported to."

"But you said this stuff was dangerous," I said.

"*Extremely* dangerous," Dad pointed out. "However, there *is* a location on the outskirts of town that has a few vials of zenoplyric acid on hand. ChemiCo Labs. Of course, they keep it under tight security. Armed guards, surveillance cameras. That kind of thing."

"So then . . . how are you going to get it?"

"Oh, we'll think of something," Dad said, a familiar gleam flashing in his eyes. "We always do."

13

Superheroes don't hang out with supervillains. And when they do, someone usually gets hurt.

"**W**anna go to the home ec room with me?" Milton asked as we stepped out into the courtyard after lunch the next day. "A reliable source tells me there might be some reject cookies from second period lying around."

I shrugged, staring down at a crack in the sidewalk.

"What's up with you?" Milton asked. "It's like you're in another world today. You can't stay focused for more than— Oooh, check it out." He pointed. "There's Sophie."

Sophie was sitting on a concrete step, eating her lunch from a brown paper sack. The instant I saw her, I made up my mind. I was going to spend the rest of my life avoiding her. Supervillains and superheroes didn't hang out with each other. And the same went for their kids.

"You're still planning to work on the project with us, right?" Milton asked. "Chilled Grease Diner after school, baby."

I'd completely forgotten that was today. It was going to be tough spending the rest of my life avoiding Sophie.

"Maybe we can do it some other time," I said. *Like never.*

"Uh . . . curly fries?" Milton prompted. "Besides, our presentation is next week. If we put it off any longer, we won't finish it."

There was no way I could tell Milton the truth, that Sophie's dad and my parents tried to kill each other on a regular basis, which made it kind of impossible for us to be friends. I had to find another way out of the group. And I had an idea.

I got to seventh period early. The room was empty except for Ms. McGirt. Her hair looked like a fluffy white cloud, and her eyes blinked up at me from behind her glasses as I approached her desk.

"Can I speak with you about something, Ms. McGirt?" I asked.

"Of course, young lady," she said.

Her eyesight must've been worse than I'd thought. At least, I hoped it was.

"It's me, Joshua," I said. "I was wondering . . . could I switch groups? Or maybe just work alone?"

Ms. McGirt gave me a long, blank stare. "I'm afraid we won't be covering the Emancipation Proclamation for another three weeks, dear."

"Uh . . . okay." This was turning out to be more difficult than I'd thought. "But—"

"If you'd like to read ahead, most of the information about Abraham Lincoln can be found in chapter eight of your textbook."

I made a few more attempts, but Ms. McGirt only responded by reciting Civil War facts and complimenting me on my makeup. Finally, I gave up and took my seat.

All throughout class, whenever Sophie looked in my direction, I buried my nose in my book. After the bell rang, she pulled me aside on the way to the Chilled Grease Diner. "What's going on?" she asked. "Why are you avoiding me?"

"I'm not avoiding you," I said, looking away.

"Oh, right." I could practically *hear* her rolling her eyes. "Does this have something to do with"—she lowered her voice—"my dad? I thought I could trust you."

Milton turned to glance back at us. "What're you guys talking about?"

"Nothing!" we both said at the same time.

Milton didn't look convinced, but he let it drop. For

the next couple of minutes, we walked in silence. Half-way through the parking lot, I felt an odd rumbling be-neath my feet.

"What was *that*?" Milton asked.

"It felt like an earthquake," I said.

"It wasn't an earthquake," Sophie said. "It was . . . something else."

"What's that supposed to mean?"

Sophie ignored me. She reached into her pocket, pulled out a cell phone, and punched a few buttons.

"If you know what's going on, you should tell us," I said to Sophie. "And who did you just call?"

"I didn't call anyone. I sent out a help signal. Now let's get out of here."

There were a lot more questions rushing around in my brain, but I had to jog to keep up with Sophie and Milton. At the next intersection, the ground began to shake again, harder this time. I grabbed hold of a traffic sign to keep from falling over.

"What *is* that?" I asked.

Sophie gave me an annoyed look. "Whatever it is that's moving around down there, it's about to attack us."

"Attack *us*? Why?"

"It just happens sometimes. It's a part of having a dad who is—" Her eyes moved to Milton. Then she looked back at me. "Anyway, I'm sure you wouldn't understand."

"I might."

"Oh, really? If you're so *understanding*, then why are you acting so weird?"

Milton was staring at us like we were speaking another language.

"Maybe I'm acting weird," I began, "because my situation is similar to your situation—but in a totally different way."

Now Milton *and* Sophie both looked lost. The ground shook. A fire hydrant on the other side of the street exploded, sending water up into the air like a geyser.

"What are you trying to say?" Sophie asked, the cell phone clutched in her hand.

I shook my head. I'd already said too much.

"Guys?" Milton pointed a quivering finger. "Something's coming out of the ground over there."

Sophie and I turned to look. A crack had formed in the middle of the intersection, like a spiderweb growing wider. Concrete crumbled and rose upward in huge blocks. A car honked and crashed into a telephone pole.

Whatever it was that had been moving around beneath us was now rising above the earth.

A silvery metallic leg broke through the concrete. Another leg emerged an instant later—then another. I watched, my heart beating furiously, as the thing pulled itself out of the hole in the street like an insect climbing out of the ground. Except this insect was the size of a golf cart, with shiny silver skin and glowing red eyes. A familiar logo was printed on one side:

Z

Firebottomed Romper™

A sickening realization crossed my mind. Whoever was controlling these things had also created the smoke creatures.

"'Firebottomed'?" Milton said. "What do you think that means?"

Before anyone could reply, the robot let out a long electronic scream. Flames shot out of its backside.

"I guess that explains it!" Milton cried.

The robotic insect let out another shriek and turned to look at us with its glowing red eyes.

"We should probably run," Sophie said.

"Good idea," I said, breaking into a jog.

We took off across the parking lot toward the football field.

"So let me see if I can get this straight," Milton said, gasping as we sprinted across the stretch of concrete. "That robot bug has spears for feet and blades for teeth, and it shoots fire out of its butt?"

"That sounds about right," I huffed.

"It must be after me," Sophie said.

"I'm not so sure about that," I said.

Sophie's feet pounded the pavement. "What are you talking about?"

This thing was connected to those smoke creatures. Meaning it was here because of *my* parents. But if I told Sophie any of this, I'd have to tell her who my parents really were. And at the moment, we had enough problems.

"On second thought," I said between deep breaths, "I bet you're right. They probably *are* here to kill you."

For some reason, this didn't seem to make her feel any better.

The earth shook again. A second later, the concrete around our feet broke open, sending Sophie tumbling to the ground.

My chest kicked with fear. There was another Romper right below us. And it was climbing to the surface.

One spindly silver leg rose up out of the hole where Sophie had just been standing. The leg landed on the ground with a sharp thud, inches from Sophie's arm.

She scrambled, trying to get to her feet, but the concrete was swaying like a wave. The robotic leg rose into the air, light reflecting off the tip of the dagger. It was pointed right at Sophie's chest.

Lunging forward just as the leg began to drop, I collided with it before the sharp tip could reach Sophie. A burst of energy flooded my veins, traveling the length of my arms and through my hands.

BOOM!

A massive explosion shot from my fingertips. It knocked the leg loose from the rest of the robot's body and sent me flying in the other direction.

When I hit the ground, I skidded across the concrete like it was a skating rink. My arms and legs stung with cuts and bruises. There were other things to worry about, though. I might've detached one of the Romper's legs, but it still had five others. Not to mention a set of deadly teeth and a butt that could burn down an entire city block.

Milton was staring at me in complete shock.

"You just . . . But how did you . . . Explosion . . ."

"The thing is," I began, "I kind of have a . . . super-power."

If it was possible, Milton looked even more dumb-founded. "What kind of superpower?"

I took a deep breath. "Spontaneous combustion."

"Spontaneous *huh*?"

"I'll explain later. Is Sophie okay?"

"I'm fine." Sophie was climbing to her feet. "Thanks for . . . you know—*that*." She gestured to the charred robot leg lying on the ground.

"No problem," I said.

"And about earlier, I'm sorry that I—"

I shook my head. "Nah. I'm the one who was acting weird. It's just that—"

115

"I'm glad you guys are working things out," Milton interrupted. "But can we talk about it later?"

He pointed. The first giant robot was still headed our way. And the second was rising out of the ground, despite the missing leg. A couple more seconds and there'd be no escaping them.

"We need to get to the football field," Sophie said.

We took off running, the Rompers trailing behind us, their legs thwacking against the pavement.

"Maybe this is a bad time," Milton panted, "but is there a reason why enormous robotic insects are chasing us?"

"I don't know," I said.

"And what about that explosion back there? I still don't get how you—"

We skidded to a stop when another earth-rumbling quake rattled beneath us. The ground opened up a few feet away. A third Romper was climbing out of the concrete.

"There are too many!" Sophie yelled. "We'll never outrun them. We've got to try something else."

"Like what?"

Sophie turned to me, her face pale. "If we get separated, I'll meet you in the center of the football field. And if one of those things attacks while I'm gone, try not to get too close to its teeth. But don't get behind it either. Because—you know—the fire."

"So stay away from both sides. Is that what you're saying?"

"Exactly." She nodded with a determined expression, her jaw set. "I'll be right back." Then Sophie took off running back in the direction we'd come from—back *toward* the Romper that was chasing us.

I watched her, my heart pounding with fear. That thing would tear Sophie apart—if it didn't burn her to a crisp first. I couldn't let her face it alone.

"I'll be right back," I said to Milton.

"Oh, no," Milton said. "Not you too."

"Just stay here."

And then I was running, chasing after Sophie. She'd nearly reached the Romper when I noticed something about her. Something different.

She was . . . glowing.

14

Every Gyft is unique in its own way.

Sophie had said that her Gyft came with a side effect. I guess this was what she'd meant.

The glow that radiated from her skin was bright, almost blinding. Looking at her was like looking at a lightbulb.

The Romper slid to a halt and pointed its rear end at Sophie. A fireball came blasting in her direction. If it had been me, I would've been roasted like a marshmallow, but Sophie whipped under the flame and grabbed hold of the robot's leg. The robot let out a surprised electronic yelp as she yanked the leg loose and plunged it into the Romper's body like a spear.

I couldn't believe what I'd just witnessed. Sophie had told me she had superhuman strength, but this was way beyond anything I'd ever imagined. By the time I caught up with her, she was shining so brightly that it hurt my eyes even to look at her. And yet I couldn't look away.

"I must look pretty strange." Her voice sounded shaky. "It only happens whenever I use my Gyft. But . . . I don't usually let other people see."

"It's okay," I said. "Really. I was just sort of—"

"Surprised to see that your project partner is the Incredible Hulk?"

"Well, technically, the Incredible Hulk is green," I pointed out. "You're more like the Incredible Lightning Bug."

Sophie shot me an angry glance as a scream ripped out across the street.

"Heeeeellllllp!"

Milton was dashing around a telephone pole, trailed by a Romper. The robot shot a burst of fire and the pole erupted into flames.

Sophie and I raced toward him. The Romper had Milton cornered against a parked car. Snapping its steel jaws, it took a bite out of Milton's backpack. The Romper was going in for the second course when Sophie reached out with both glowing hands and snapped the thing's head from its body like it was an oversized doll.

The headless Romper swayed for a moment, let out a final puff of fire from its backside, and then collapsed.

"Are you okay?" Sophie asked Milton.

He looked at us with large, wet eyes. Broken pieces of metal and concrete were stuck to his hair. He spoke in a droopy, faraway voice.

"I. Just. Wanted. Curly. Fries."

He definitely sounded a little shaken up, but I figured he'd recover.

Milton nudged me with his elbow. "Is she . . . glowing?"

I nodded.

"Okay." He sounded relieved. "At least you can see it too."

"Come on," Sophie said. "We've got to get to that football field."

"Why?" I asked. The concrete shook. More Rompers were rising from the ground all around us.

"That's where Stanley's picking us up."

"Who's Stanley?"

"Our ride."

We sprinted across the parking lot, dodging rising Rompers.

"Just out of curiosity," Milton said, breathing heavily as he ran, "what happened back there? 'Cause it looked like you"—he turned to me—"created an explosion out of midair. And you"—he told Sophie—"just ripped the head off a killer robot insect?"

Sophie's only response was to point out a section of the parking lot ahead of us where a Romper was rising from the ground. Without slowing down, she swung her foot and kicked the thing's head clear off its body.

"Am I the only one here without a superpower?" Milton asked.

We kept running. The field was getting closer. The entrance was locked shut, but I figured we'd deal with that when we got there. Firebottomed Rompers clawed across the parking lot, closing in on us.

On the gate at the entrance to the field, a sign read:

NO ENTRY WITHOUT AUTHORIZATION

"I'll take care of this," I said.

Grabbing hold of the lock, I closed my eyes and attempted to block out all sound. My concentration evaporated when Sophie's voice broke in.

"Are you sure you don't want me to help?" she asked.

"Just give me a second," I said. "I can do it." I wanted to prove that I could—to her, and to myself.

I closed my eyes again as a feeling came over me—strange and familiar at the same time. A tingling in my fingers. Heart pounding. All of a sudden, the lock in my hand felt like a pot of boiling water, but I kept a firm grip until I heard the sound of exploding metal. The lock burst apart, and the gate swung open.

We pushed through the entryway and kept running, passing beneath the bleachers and emerging onto the football field. Behind me, I heard a sound that caused a shiver of fear to run down my spine. The Rompers had torn through the fence. They were charging the field behind us.

"Are you sure your ride's gonna make it?" I asked.

"Don't worry," she said. "Stanley will come."

"Did he say *when* he was planning to show up?" Milton glanced back nervously as the first of the Rompers stepped onto the field.

"There he is!" Sophie exclaimed, pointing up.

Above us, a black hover SUV was descending toward the center of the field. A pile of loose grass and dust swept up around the sides of the SUV as it came to rest on the ground.

We took off running again. The sound of the Rompers trailed behind us, their sharp legs and flaming butts turning the football field into a disaster zone.

The doors of the hover SUV swung open. Milton was the first inside. Then Sophie. I dove in after her, landing on top of them both. The door closed behind me. An instant later, a Romper crashed against the outside of the SUV. There was a dull thud, but the SUV remained in one piece.

"Don't worry," Sophie said. "The car is titanium re-inforced and armor plated. Nothing's getting through."

She was right. The SUV shook a little, but that was all the Rompers could do. It was like going through the automatic car wash. Except instead of soapy rags and brushes, our car was surrounded by bursts of flame and sharp metallic legs.

Something moved in the front seat. My heart leaped into my throat as I realized that one of the robots had made it into the SUV.

"Good afternoon, children."

It took me another split second to realize what was happening. The thing in the front seat *was* a robot, but not the kind that had attacked us. It had a silver human-like face, and bulging eyes the color of pearls. It was wearing a chauffeur's hat and a black suit.

"Guys," Sophie said, "this is Stanley. My butler, driver, and bodyguard. All rolled into one."

It was my first time meeting a robotic butler/driver/bodyguard, and I wasn't sure quite how to act.

"Um . . . hi," I said.

"Yo." Milton saluted.

The SUV continued rocking back and forth from the impact of the Rompers outside.

"Thanks for coming on such short notice, Stanley," Sophie said. Her skin was already losing its glow. "We need to go someplace where those things won't be able to attack us. Someplace secure." She hesitated, then said, "Take us back to the house, Stanley."

"Very well, Miss Justice."

"Did he just call you . . . 'Miss Justice'?" Milton looked from Sophie to Stanley and back again. I could see the pieces coming together in his mind. All the gossip we'd heard from the Cafeteria Girls, the superpower, the titanium-walled vehicle. "Does that mean you're . . . ?"

Sophie nodded.

"And that your dad is . . . ?"

Sophie nodded again.

"And we're about to . . . ?"

Sophie kept on nodding.

Milton's eyes went wide. All the Captain Justice trading cards he carried around with him, the Captain Justice sheets on his bed, the copies of *Super Scoop* with Captain Justice's face plastered across the cover. And now he was sharing a hover SUV with the superhero's daughter.

It was his dream come true.

I wasn't quite so excited. As flames blossomed against the fireproof windows, I thought about all the things my parents had said about Captain Justice. That he was a know-nothing do-gooder. A corporate sellout. A mortal enemy.

And now we were on our way to his house.

15

Captain Justice has ranked at the top of the Annual List of Highest-Paid Superheroes eight years in a row. During his career, he's shown that he is willing to endorse just about any product that will pay him.

I f you ignored the robot driver and the fact that we were flying a thousand feet above the ground, the hover SUV looked like the inside of pretty much any other car.

Milton was leaning forward in his seat, talking excitedly to Stanley about what it was like to work for Captain Justice. By now, Sophie had returned to her normal non-glowing self.

"What *was* that back there?" I asked.

"I don't know," Sophie said. "I've never seen anything like them before. My guess is they were sent by the

Dread Duo. Probably trying to get back at my dad for what happened a few weeks ago."

"You don't know that," I blurted out.

Sophie gave me a surprised look. "Dr. Dread is an inventor. He probably built those things and programmed them to attack me. You know, as revenge or something."

"All I'm saying is that we shouldn't just *assume* it was the Dread Duo."

"And *I'm* just saying it would make sense if it *was* the Dread Duo. They've been trying to kill my dad for at least the last ten years."

"Well . . . I bet they had their reasons," I said in a voice that was sharper than I'd intended. I knew I should have just left it alone, but I could feel defensiveness flaring up inside me. "Anyway, it's not like your dad never tried to kill the Dread Duo."

"What's *that* supposed to mean?"

All of a sudden, I couldn't stand looking at Sophie. Just because my parents were supervillains, and just because they sometimes tried to destroy the world— that didn't mean she had to go around blaming them for everything bad that happened.

Anyway, I *knew* the Firebottomed Rompers hadn't been there for Sophie. The logo on the side meant that there had to be some connection to the smoke creatures. But who was behind all this?

When Milton was done talking with Stanley, he turned around in his seat and gave me a long look.

"So you've got a superpower, huh?" he said. "And you never thought to tell *me*?"

"I haven't known for very long," I said.

"Uh-huh. But you already told Sophie, right?"

"Well . . . yeah."

"Interesting." Milton crossed his arms in front of his chest. "*Very* interesting."

"What?" I could feel my face going red.

"It just seems like the kind of thing best friends tell each other. I would definitely let you know if *I* had simultaneous combustion."

"*Spontaneous* combustion."

"Whatever." Milton stared out the window at the passing clouds.

"Look, I'm sorry. I guess I was embarrassed. I didn't want you to think I was some kind of freak."

Milton scrunched up his face. "Freak? I think it's awesome you have a superpower! The way you made that Romper's leg explode . . . It was probably the coolest thing I've ever seen in real life! Just as long as you're not keeping any other big secrets I don't know about."

My heart sank. *Any other big secrets?* Like maybe a fake identity? Parents who tried to destroy the world every couple of months? Did those count as big secrets?

Sophie's house appeared from within a cluster of trees below. You couldn't miss it. The place was enormous. I'd heard the Cafeteria Girls say it was big, but I'd had no idea it was *this* big. Imagine the largest house you've ever seen. Now imagine that someone took five or six of the largest houses you've ever seen and attached them together, then surrounded all of it with a moat and then surrounded *that* with a security wall and a lookout tower armed with machine guns. That might give you some idea of what Sophie's house looked like.

"We should be safe from those Rompers here," Sophie said.

"Looks like it," I said.

In front of us, Stanley pressed a button on the dashboard, and the roof of the garage opened. The hover SUV drifted downward.

The vehicle came to rest on the floor of the garage. The roof slowly closed above us. Stepping out of the SUV, I looked across the vast space. At home, our garage was a mess of tools and half-assembled gadgets lying around on workbenches, jars of flesh-eating bacteria gathering dust on the shelves, basketballs and bicycles and hover scooters pushed into the corners.

This garage was a huge space, at least fifty times larger than our garage at home. Dozens of vehicles of all kinds were arranged in rows. Sports cars, luxury sedans, armored tanks. I couldn't believe that they all belonged to one person.

Parked next to the hover SUV was a red convertible, glistening and new. The license plate read:

JUSTICE

We followed Stanley through the garage, between rows of shining vehicles, until we reached a door at the far end of the room. Stanley held out his hand. When it neared the doorknob, a silver key popped out from the end of his finger. He inserted the key into the lock and turned. The door opened.

"By the way," Sophie said, "when you see my dad, try not to mention that we almost got killed by giant robotic insect monsters, okay?"

"Why not?" I asked. "It seems like the kind of thing he might want to know about."

"He's a little obsessed with my safety."

I thought back to the moat surrounding the house and the machine guns on the guard towers surrounding the moat. She had a point.

"If my dad thinks I'm in danger," she went on, "then we might have to move again." Her eyes found me in the gloom of the garage. "And I'd kind of like to stay."

I followed Sophie through the doorway into a vast marble-tiled room. An oriental rug stretched across the floor at our feet. A staircase curved upward in front of us. The room was bigger than an average house. And this was just the entryway.

"May I fetch you a refreshing beverage?" Stanley asked.

"Uh, sure." Milton glanced over at Sophie, and when she nodded, he turned back to the robot. "That sounds great."

"What would you like, sir?"

"Do you have Dr Pepper?"

"Affirmative. How many would you like?"

"Umm . . . how many can I have?"

"Please allow me one moment while I compute your request."

For a couple of seconds, the only sound coming out of the robot was a low rumble. Milton stared at him, his eyes beaming.

"A human life-form of your size and weight is capable of consuming 314.65 liquid ounces of Dr Pepper in a two-hour period," Stanley said. "That equals 26.22 cans. You should be warned that evidence from medical studies has shown that such excessive overconsumption of fructose-based carbonated water could result in severe illness and—"

"I'll take twenty-six cans, please," Milton said.

I elbowed Milton.

"Er—actually, I'll just take one."

"Me too," I said.

"Just water for me," Sophie said.

"Very well," said Stanley. He bowed mechanically, then strolled jerkily across the room.

"We're still getting moved in," Sophie said, pointing at a pile of cardboard boxes. "Stanley's in the process of unpacking everything."

"So," Milton said, "is your . . . er . . . dad actually . . . here?"

"Yeah," Sophie said.

"Now?"

"I think so."

Milton looked like he couldn't decide whether to scream or faint. "Cool," he said.

Sophie led us deeper into the house. We passed through a living room, a sitting room, a solarium, a dining room, another living room, a kitchen, a library, a third living room, and several other rooms that didn't seem to have any purpose at all.

One room looked like some kind of art gallery. Oil paintings hung on the walls, encased in flamboyant gold frames, all showing portraits of the same person: Captain Justice.

Another room was filled with merchandise. Boxes of cereal, shelves of tennis shoes, watches, T-shirts, toys. It took me a moment to realize what all the products had in common: They were all endorsed by Captain Justice.

It was the room where he displayed all his merchandise deals. It seemed like a weird thing for a person to have in his own house. On the other hand, I supposed that Captain Justice had to do *something* with all those rooms.

I picked up a box of Frosted Fuel Flakes with Captain Justice's picture on it. The box was empty. So was a nearby box of microwavable burritos. On the label was a picture of Captain Justice wearing a sombrero. The text underneath read: *You can be a hero too with Señor Loco's Three-Minute Mexican Feast!*

This must've been what the Cafeteria Girls had been talking about. Shelf after shelf of empty boxes. All with Captain Justice plastered across the label.

At the far end of the room was a life-sized cardboard cutout of Captain Justice. He looked just like he did in real life. He was grinning his perfect grin, showing off his perfect teeth and his perfect hair. A shiny blue cape hung around his muscular neck. One hand was giving a thumbs-up, while the other was clutching a stick of beef jerky. Beneath him was a label:

Justice Jerky®
A super way to feel good and keep fit!!!

We walked into the next room, and there was Captain Justice again. Except this time, it wasn't a cardboard cutout.

It was the real thing.

He wasn't wearing his usual silver and blue uniform. Instead, he was dressed in a silver tracksuit and matching headband.

The room was full of bulky machinery that looked designed to inflict some serious pain. Sharp claws, leather straps, spinning knobs. The Cafeteria Girls had been right. They looked just like high-tech torture devices.

And Captain Justice was strapped into one of them.

16

Meeting a superhero in real life can be an unforgettable experience.

Captain Justice's hands were grasped by mechanical levers. His feet were hooked up to rotating pedals. Devious-looking robotic arms gripped him around the waist and neck.

That was when I realized Captain Justice wasn't being tortured. He was exercising.

The machine moved around him, a whirring hive of spinning silver parts. Captain Justice's legs swung back and forth on the rotating pedals while he simultaneously heaved a barbell up and down with his arms. As if that weren't enough, he was also attached to straps that stretched and pulled and twisted different parts of his body into various yoga positions.

Milton gasped. He was in the same room as his hero. And his hero seemed to be doing the weirdest exercises any of us had ever seen.

"Hi, Dad," Sophie said, walking across the room.

"Hello, Daughter!" Captain Justice managed to say between deep breaths.

"How's it going?"

"Marvelous! The lab just came up with this machine last week, and it's wonderfully efficient. It allows me to do all my different exercises at once. In fifteen minutes!"

I watched in awed silence as Captain Justice jogged and lifted weights and performed the downward-facing dog pose, all at the same time.

"These are my friends." Sophie nodded to the two of us. "Milton and Joshua."

A flash of panic flared up in my chest. What if Captain Justice recognized me as the son of the Dread Duo? If he had tracked my parents to Sheepsdale, he might also know about me.

But Captain Justice didn't seem to notice me, or much of anything outside his exercise machine. "Greetings, local children!" was all he said. He turned to smile at us, but then the machine grabbed his neck and yanked him into a new position.

"H-hello, Captain Justice," Milton said nervously. "I

CAPTAIN JUSTICE

Captain Justice can fly over skyscrapers, juggle boulders, and summon an entire arsenal of holo-weapons. When he isn't battling the world's worst bad guys, he can usually be found endorsing some of the world's bestselling products.

j-just wanted to say that it is an honor and a . . . a thrill to meet you today."

His hand trembling, Milton reached into his backpack—or what remained of his backpack. The Fire-bottomed Romper had taken a pretty significant bite out of it. From a tangle of ripped papers and books, he removed a magazine that was still in pretty good shape. Glancing at the cover, I instantly recognized the splashy colors and the bold headlines. It was the new issue of *Super Scoop*.

Milton took a step forward, clasping the magazine close to his chest. Captain Justice continued to huff and jog and heave and twist.

"Um . . . Mr.—I mean, *Captain* Justice," Milton began, "I was wondering, if it isn't too much trouble, if you might be able to . . . to sign an autograph for me."

"Most certainly!"

Milton held the magazine out with one hand, a pen gripped in the other. A mechanical arm swung out from the exercise machine and grabbed the pen. With a quick, robotic motion, the device scribbled something onto the cover.

"See what I mean?" Captain Justice said as the machine signed his autograph for him. "This really improves my efficiency!"

When the machine was done with the autograph, it attempted to return the pen to Milton, though it looked more like it was trying to stab him in the face. Milton ducked just in time. The pen fell to the ground. Captain Justice went on with his exercise.

"Wow!" Milton gushed. "Thanks, Captain Justice!"

"You're welcome, Marlon! Just don't believe everything you read in that magazine." Captain Justice nodded at the copy of *Super Scoop*. In the next instant, the machine prodded him into a new and torturous position. "A couple of weeks ago, they claimed I was having a secret relationship with Scarlett Flame just because some paparazzi caught us talking together for five minutes outside my agent's office. On the other hand, *Super Scoop* is a terrific platform for promotion. My business manager tells me that it reaches a key demographic of—"

"That's great, Dad," Sophie interrupted. "I was going to show them the rest of the house."

"Of course, darling!" Captain Justice said. "Enjoy your afternoon!"

Milton would've been happy to stand at Captain Justice's side for as long as possible, but Sophie was already guiding us out of the room. She led us through an arched doorway, down a hall, and up a winding stairway.

"I can't believe Captain Justice gave me his autograph!" Milton whispered to me as we climbed the stairs.

"Well, technically it's his exercise machine's autograph," I said.

"I know. It's amazing!" He held out the magazine,

admiring the fresh new signature. I stopped walking when my eyes moved from the autograph to another part of the cover. In the right-hand corner was an image of a smoke creature. Next to it was a section of bold text that read:

MORE VILLAINS GO MISSING!

My chest tightened. I stared at the photograph of the smoke creature. The image was dark and slightly out of focus, but it was definitely the same thing that had attacked at the Vile Fair.

All the websites about the super community were discussing it too. There'd been dozens more attacks by smoke creatures in the weeks since the Vile Fair. They appeared in supervillains' homes, or interrupted them in the middle of their evil plots. And each time, it was always the same. The smoke surrounded its victim. A burst of lightning filled the cloud. And then—gone.

All of a sudden it felt like someone had turned down the thermostat in Sophie's house by twenty degrees. I couldn't help thinking about my parents. They were close to tracking down whoever was controlling these things. But what would happen if the smoke came for them first?

"You coming?" Sophie's voice echoed in the marble stairway. She and Milton were at the top of the steps, looking down at me.

I did my best to choke down the knot in my throat and followed them.

Sophie led us down another winding corridor, in and out of grand rooms that were mostly empty or piled with unpacked cardboard boxes. At the end of a long hallway, Sophie pushed open the door to her bedroom.

The room wasn't very big, considering how huge the rest of the house was. There was a desk in the corner, piled with papers and books. A pair of jeans was draped over a nearby chair. Several framed photographs were hanging on the wall, displaying snow-covered trees, tall rock formations rising from the beach, an old brownstone apartment with boarded-up windows.

Milton immediately began examining one of the photos—a close-up shot of a strand of grass, with a row of buildings in the background.

"Did these pictures, like, come with the frames?" he asked.

Sophie looked back at him, offended.

"No!" she said.

"Oh. 'Cause they're really good. I thought they must've been professional."

The annoyed look on Sophie's face vanished. "I took those photographs," she said. For a split second, I thought her power was kicking in again. But she wasn't glowing this time. She was blushing.

"Wow! You *took* these?" Milton looked genuinely impressed. "That's really cool. Whenever I take pictures, they always come out too dark or blurry or everyone has red eyes. But these are great."

"I have a pretty good camera and lens. That makes a difference. And my mom was a professional photographer. So . . ."

Sophie's voice trailed away. It was the first time she'd ever mentioned her mom.

"I took that one a couple of weeks ago," she said, pointing to the photo of grass and buildings. "That was the day we moved to Sheepsdale. My dad was in meetings all day, so Stanley took me out to the park with my camera."

This brought a smile to Sophie's face again. I got the feeling she smiled a lot when the subject turned to photography.

We settled at Sophie's desk to work on our project.

"I'm gonna have trouble explaining *this*." Milton pulled the remains of our history book out of his mangled backpack. The cover had been ripped away and half the pages were shredded. His notebook was in even worse shape. "Do you think my teachers will believe me if I tell them a Firebottomed Romper ate my homework?"

"I have another copy of that book," Sophie said. "In the library."

"I'll get it," I said.

"Are you sure? This house can be like a maze some-times."

"I know exactly where it is."

Sophie still looked skeptical, but I was already on my feet and halfway across the room. I was looking for an excuse to search around a little on my own. Growing up in a house with supervillains, I'd always wondered what a superhero's home would look like. So far, all I knew was that it was much—*much*—bigger.

"Just take a left at the end of the hallway, then down the stairs, into a room where you'll see a marble dog beside a tall fireplace, into another hallway, and then you take the third door on your right," Sophie told me. "Got it?"

I nodded, trying to keep all the directions straight in my head. Left, down the stairs, marble dog, hallway, third door on the right. No problem.

At least, that was what I thought. It took me only a minute of wandering around before I got completely lost. Stumbling from one room to the next, I eventually found myself standing in front of a wall that was entirely covered with televisions. Each showed a different video image of an ordinary scene—a street or a sidewalk or a park.

I stood there, hypnotized. The one nearest to me was of a man walking his dog along a sidewalk, obviously unaware that he was being watched. The dog sniffed a bush, then scratched itself. Its owner began scratching himself as well.

It was just like the Cafeteria Girls had said. Each television was hooked up to some kind of surveillance video. I watched as the man and his dog continued to scratch themselves.

And that was when I heard the sounds of someone entering the room next door. Footsteps. Then a voice.

Peering around the corner, I saw Captain Justice standing at the far end of the room. He was facing the other direction, still wearing his silver exercise outfit, having a conversation with an enormous disembodied head.

17

Many years ago, superheroes were mostly vigilantes in spandex tights. Now they're highly trained media figures. In tights.

The head was a hologram. Pale blue, flickering like a ghost, it was floating in the air in front of Captain Justice.

"I have some unpleasant news," said the hologram.

"What is it, Fink?" Captain Justice asked.

"The trend data we've gathered shows that your popularity is declining."

"Declining? In which demographics?"

"All of them."

Captain Justice slumped forward. "What about the

four- to eight-year-old female demographic? I thought you said that was a growing market."

"Our research has shown that girls under eight don't relate to you," said the hologram named Fink. "They prefer softer, gentler forms of merchandizing. Dolls, kittens, boy bands—that kind of thing."

"What can I do to change this?"

"We're working on a plush toy. Part of the Huggable Heroes line. Unfortunately, we've hit a snag in product testing. It seems that the Huggable Captain Justice is more popular as a chew toy for dogs than as a plaything for young girls."

"A chew toy? Is that profitable?"

"Absolutely. Pet merchandizing is a booming market. We're already looking into the Captain Justice Scratching Post and Fun Time Climbing Station for Adventurous Cats. Litter box included."

"Hmm, yes. I see." Captain Justice scratched under his headband. "Well, if you think there's a market, we should pursue it."

"Glad to hear you're on board, Captain J!"

"What about the other project? I presume you're still keeping it a secret."

Fink nodded his enormous disembodied blue head.

"I'm the only member of the staff who knows about it at this point."

"Good. Let's keep it that way. We don't want any of this to leak to the media. Not until we're ready to make our announcement."

"That's why we're moving the operation to our remote location. We should be able to continue our work there without interruption."

"How do you think the public will react to such a different strategy?"

"It may take some time for people to get used to the change," Fink said, "but it's a step in the right direction, believe me."

"You don't think it's too . . . aggressive?"

"The world is a more aggressive place, Captain J. You're just adjusting to the times."

Captain Justice paused, as if he still wasn't quite convinced. I leaned forward, curiosity stirring inside me. What kind of project were they talking about? And why keep it so secret? From everything I knew about Captain Justice, he wasn't the kind of guy who ever refused media attention.

I might've leaned a little too far into the room, because for a second I was sure that Fink noticed me. His enormous blue eyes swiveled until he seemed to be looking right at me. I darted behind the corner, clutching my chest as if I could cover the sound of my own pounding heart. Had he seen me? Could a holographic head even *see* that far? Either way, I didn't want to stick around to find out. Stepping as softly as possible, I crept backward and out of the room.

$$✤$$

"What took you so long?" Milton asked when I finally found my way back to Sophie's room. But since he'd just stuffed his mouth full of Justice Jerky, it came out sounding like "Whaa ookk ooh soo ong?"

My heart was still pounding from the sight of Fink's enormous blue head. I had no idea what he'd been talking about with Captain Justice, but I decided to keep it to myself.

"I just got a little turned around," I explained. I handed him the history book. Luckily, I'd managed to find the library on my way back.

"I told you this house can be confusing," Sophie said. "I still get lost too."

Milton reached into the half-empty bag of Justice Jerky on the desk next to him and took another huge bite. "Waahsum eef urkee?" he asked.

Translation: "Want some beef jerky?"

Sophie shot him a disgusted look. "Didn't anyone ever tell you not to talk with your mouth full?"

Milton shrugged, his cheeks bulging. "Buh iss eelithous!"

"What?"

Milton swallowed. "But it's delicious." He gave the bag of Justice Jerky an appreciative squeeze. "Seriously, your dad makes the best beef jerky in the world."

Sophie rolled her eyes. "It's not like he actually *makes* the stuff. They just slap his name and face onto the package."

"Whatever," Milton said, shoving another handful into his mouth.

A couple of hours later, Stanley offered to drive us home and Sophie insisted on coming with us. "In case there are any more attacks," she said.

We took the hover SUV again, although this time we stuck to the roads. After exiting the garage, the SUV traveled down a wooded path, past surveillance cameras, and over the moat. Stanley drove through the security gate, and soon we were on the road, heading into town.

When we came to a halt at a red light, I glanced out my window and saw something that made me seriously wish we'd taken another route.

My parents.

They were decked out in full supervillain regalia. Mom had on her green body armor and black mask. Dad was wearing the massive silver goggles that he put on only when he was in the middle of pulling off one of his horrible schemes.

They were standing near the entrance to a two-story office building. Attached to the roof of the building was a sign that read CHEMICO LABS, INC. My parents had mentioned ChemiCo Labs last night. That was where the zenoplyric acid was being held, the deadly chemical that could help them track where the smoke creatures were transporting villains.

So that was what they were doing. They were there to get that acid.

I recalled the sly look on my dad's face when I'd asked him how they planned to get their hands on the chemical. *Oh, we'll think of something,* he'd said. *We always do.*

Apparently, this is what he'd meant by "something."

The building was surrounded by a tall chain-link fence that was topped by barbed wire. It looked like my parents had rounded up all the employees. People in lab coats and security uniforms huddled in the parking lot. Mom raised one hand, and a vine untangled itself from the wall of the building. The vine snaked forward, levitating under her control, and wrapped around the group.

Dad removed a device from his belt, clicking a button that caused the device to unfold like a miniature satellite dish. I'd seen the gadget before. It was one of Dad's own inventions. The Dread Deactomatic. When he pulled the trigger, it deactivated all the electronic gadgetry in the crowd, making cell phones and walkie-talkies useless. Meanwhile, Mom confiscated the security guards' weapons.

A movement at the edge of the parking lot caught my attention. A gray, disheveled figure was staggering close to the barbed wire fence. Another had emerged from the side of the building. Zombies. My parents must've brought them along as an extra precaution.

I wasn't the only one who'd noticed what was going on outside ChemiCo Labs. Milton and Sophie were crowded next to the window, pointing at the scene.

"The Dread Duo's breaking into that building!" Milton said. "And they have zombies! Cool!"

I clenched my teeth together. "We really should be going. It might be dangerous."

But nobody in the car was listening to me. Sophie dug into her pocket for her cell phone. "I need to call my dad."

"Why get parents involved?" I said in a too-loud voice. "Your dad's probably busy. Ooh, look—the light's green. You can go now, Stanley."

But Stanley kept his robotic foot on the brake. "I believe Sophie is correct," he said. "Captain Justice prefers to be informed about any sighting of the Dread Duo."

It would probably take Captain Justice a few minutes to get dressed. Plus another minute or so travel time. Meaning my parents had maybe five minutes—at most—before their little party was interrupted. And I really didn't want to relive the scene from the other week.

I unlocked the backseat door and was out on the pavement in a second. Sophie and Milton called out to me, but their voices were nothing more than a blur in the background.

I nearly got flattened by a minivan while I was bolting across the street, but I managed to get to the curb. When I reached the fence, I thrust out my arms. A current of energy pulsed through my hands, and a charred hole formed, big enough to climb through.

I was ducking through the gap in the fence when Sophie came running up behind me.

"Joshua, are you crazy?" The fence clattered as she climbed through after me. "The Dread Duo will kill you."

"No, they won't."

"How can you be so sure?"

"I just . . . am."

Sophie stared back at me, waiting. But there was no way I could tell her the truth—not without also telling her who my parents really were—so I decided on plan B instead.

"You and Milton need to get out of here!" I said in a harsh voice. "I'll be fine. Now—go!"

Sophie only shook her head, her jaw clenched fiercely. A second later, Milton caught up with us, gasping for breath. "No way we're letting you go in there by yourself," he said.

Everything was happening too quickly. There wasn't any time to try to talk them out of following me. But bringing them along didn't seem like such a good option either. And any minute now, Captain Justice was going to show up.

Just when I thought the situation couldn't get any worse, it did. One of the zombies was glaring at us from behind its lifeless red eyes. Then it began staggering in our direction.

"That doesn't look good," Milton said.

An awful growl ricocheted across the parking lot. The zombie was getting closer.

An idea lodged itself in my mind. I wasn't sure whether it would work, but we were out of options.

"Milton! Do you still have any of that beef jerky on you?"

He blinked. "I might've taken a few for the road. Why?"

"Give it to me. Quick."

Milton reached into his pockets and pulled out a handful of Justice Jerky. "Here you go. But this hardly seems like the time for a snack."

The zombie's dragging footsteps grew louder. Was it my imagination, or had I just caught a whiff of its rancid breath?

Doing my best to keep my hands from shaking, I unwrapped the sticks of jerky, then held them up.

"Uh . . . Joshua?" I could hear the anxiety in Sophie's voice. "What are you doing?"

"Just something my mom showed me. She knows all sorts of tricks for dealing with zombies."

As soon as I'd said it, I realized how strange that must've sounded. But it was too late now. The zombie was only a few feet away. I began waving the jerky back and forth. The zombie stopped, and a hungry look passed over its gray features. Its dull eyes followed the jerky like a dog watching a ball about to be thrown.

"You want the Justice Jerky?" I said.

I couldn't be sure, but the zombie seemed to nod. Its mouth was open, revealing a mouthful of rotten teeth.

"You *sure* you want the Justice Jerky?"

The zombie was now hopping up and down eagerly.

"Then go get it!" I tossed the handful of jerky as far as I could across the parking lot.

The zombie spun around and shuffled after it.

Before Sophie and Milton could ask any questions, I took off running. My parents were no longer standing in the parking lot. They must've gotten inside the building by now, and were searching for the acid.

The tied-up group of scientists and security guards watched as I went running past.

"Hey, kid—wait!" a woman yelled. "Don't go in there!"

The woman's voice blurred into the background. Through the glass double doors I could see my parents.

And something was wrong. I could tell from their faces. Mom took a quick step forward, then backed up again. Dad's hand inched closer to his utility belt.

It was like they were cornered, trapped on all sides. But by what? All I could see were shadows at the edges of the lobby.

And then one of the shadows moved. Dark shapes shifted out of the corners of the lobby, moving closer to my parents.

It was as if the shadows were alive.

A wave of terror swept over me. Smoke creatures. There were four of them. And they had my parents surrounded.

I pushed on the door, but it wouldn't budge. My parents must've locked it from the inside. Through the glass, I watched as Dad raised the Deactomatic. For a split second, I felt my heart leap. But before Dad could pull the trigger, one of the creatures lunged forward and knocked the device out of his hand.

Every last ounce of my hope trickled away. My parents were powerless. I could hear their muffled screams on the other side of the door as the smoke creatures swirled around them like storm clouds.

Panic flashed through my mind. I slammed my fists against the double doors, and my spontaneous combustion did the rest. The door exploded into a million glass shards.

I rushed into the lobby, the surge of energy still throbbing in my veins, just in time to see the last trace of my parents vanish behind the dark smoke. There were two flashes of light this time—one for each of them—bursts of lightning from within the chaos of clouds.

In the next moment, the smoke creatures were gone.

And so were my parents.

18

**Many Gyfted children follow
in their parents' footsteps.**

The sound of my scream echoed through the lobby. I felt suddenly as though a hole had been ripped open inside of me and everything that had ever mattered was falling through it. One second, my parents were there, struggling with the smoke creatures. And then— nothing.

Behind me I heard the sound of footsteps crunching over broken glass. Sophie came running into the lobby. The moment we looked at each other, I saw recognition in her eyes.

"The Dread Duo," she said. "They're—"

"My parents." I nodded. "Yeah."

Now that the truth was finally out there, I didn't feel any of the emotions I would've expected—no fear or shame or even embarrassment.

I just felt empty.

And Sophie didn't react the way I'd expected either. I'd figured she might be angry or shocked. But all she did was gaze back at me sympathetically.

"I'm sorry," she whispered.

A second later, Milton stepped carefully through the broken doorway. "What happened?" He glanced expectantly around the empty lobby. "What'd I miss?"

"My parents were just attacked," I said, staring into the empty space where they'd just been. "They're gone."

"What d'you mean? The Dread Duo kidnapped your parents?"

"No, Milton." I shook my head. "The Dread Duo. They *are* my parents."

I'd spent the previous twelve years hiding their identity, and now I'd just confessed the truth twice in one minute. If Milton was freaked out that he'd been living down the street from two of the world's worst villains, he didn't show it.

Instead, he only blinked and asked, "What happened to them?"

I told Sophie and Milton what my parents had told

me—about the smoke creatures, the nano-beings, super-villains getting transported.

"Transported *where*?" Sophie asked.

I shook my head, staring at the glass shards around my feet. "I don't know. There's only one way to track them. And to do that, I'd need—"

The chemical compound my parents had been trying to steal. Zenoplyric acid. And we just happened to be in the lobby of the one place in Sheepsdale where you could actually *get* it. My parents had mentioned that the lab was normally well guarded. But at the moment, all the employees and armed security guards were still tied up outside. Meaning that we had the building all to ourselves.

I started running across the empty lobby. I knew what needed to be done.

Sophie and Milton called out after me. "Wait, Joshua! What're you doing?"

I turned around, my heart beating in my chest like an engine in overdrive.

"I'm going to steal a deadly chemical!"

I'd never stolen anything in my life. That was more my parents' area of expertise. And I definitely never would've considered breaking into a heavily secured laboratory to steal a vial of dangerous acid.

At least, not until now.

There were no other options. The only way I'd ever be able to find my parents was to get my hands on that chemical. Besides, my mom and dad had already done most of the hard work for me. All I had to do was find the stuff.

We didn't have much time. Any minute, Captain Justice would show up and untie everyone outside. The entire building would return to lockdown mode, and any chance of finding my parents would vanish.

Milton and Sophie trailed me down a long corridor, past empty guard stations. When I reached an elevator, I stopped and looked back at them.

"You guys should turn around," I said between heavy breaths. "I can handle it from here."

"We're not leaving you," Sophie said.

"Yeah," Milton huffed. "We want to help."

I shook my head. "This chemical I'm looking for—it's rare. And dangerous."

"But you need it, right?" Sophie asked. "You can use it to get your parents back?"

"Yeah. I hope so."

"Then maybe we should split up."

I stared back at her. Sophie—Captain Justice's

daughter—was offering to help *me*? Even after finding out who my parents were?

Milton stepped forward. "She's right. This building is huge. If we split up, we'll be able to cover more ground."

I gave Sophie a sharp look. "Your dad probably wouldn't approve."

"Our parents' problems are between them," Sophie said. "You're my friend. And I want to help."

As much as I hated the idea of dragging my friends into this, they *did* have a point. The building was huge, and we'd have a much better chance of finding what we were looking for with three people looking instead of one.

"Okay," I said. "Here's what we do."

We decided that Milton would explore the rest of the first floor, while Sophie and I would divide up the second floor. If anyone spotted us, we could just say that we'd gotten lost trying to hide from the Dread Duo.

"We'll meet up outside," I said, pressing the elevator button. The doors slid open.

"Wait," Milton said as Sophie and I entered the elevator. "What are we looking for again?"

"Zenoplyric acid."

"And how do I know if I've found it?"

I thought about this for a second. "I don't know. I was kind of hoping it would be labeled."

Milton looked like he had about a thousand questions

160

he still wanted to ask, but the doors slid closed between us before he had a chance.

Sophie and I were alone in the elevator. Except for the smooth jazz saxophone playing softly in the speakers, it was silent. My entire body felt coiled with uncertainty. When the doors opened at the second floor, Sophie and I gave each other one last look.

"Good luck," she said.

"You too."

Then we set off in opposite directions. Soon the only sound was the squeak of my footsteps against the floor and the rhythm of my breathing.

I explored one room after another, looking across walls of lab equipment, opening cabinets, checking the labels of every chemical I came across. But I couldn't find the zenoplyric acid anywhere.

I was beginning to wonder whether my parents had made a mistake—whether the chemical was even here at all—when I heard a sudden beep behind me. Spinning around, I saw sensors lining the door I'd just passed through. A pair of heavy steel doors dropped down on either end of the room, blocking the entrance and exit.

A second later, the alarm went off.

19

**In a stressful situation, it's best
to remain calm. Sometimes help comes
from the most unexpected places.**

I was trapped.

With the siren ringing in my ears, I frantically surveyed my surroundings. It was a laboratory, similar to a dozen others I'd passed through already. The only escape routes I could see were the doors at both ends of the room, and they'd just been closed off by solid steel barriers.

I slammed my fists against the hard steel surface and tried to concentrate my power on blasting my way through. But the barricade was way too thick, and the only thing that felt like it was going to explode was my head. The wailing alarm was like a police siren in my brain.

I searched the walls for a control box that might shut off the security system. Nothing. I checked the air vent for an escape, but the slim passageway was barely wide enough for someone half my size.

I could feel the last glimmer of hope fading. Any chance of rescuing my parents would soon be gone. Would I ever see them again? What was I supposed to do if I couldn't get my parents back? Where would I live?

I glanced around the room for something—anything—I could use to get out. Circling the room, I opened drawers and cabinets, uncovering loose wires, old scientific journals, vials of chemicals—

Vials of chemicals?

The glass vials were arranged in neat rows across a long metal rack. Each was filled with a colored liquid and labeled with the name of a chemical component I'd never heard of. Except for one. A cloudy blue liquid near the middle of the rack. I recognized the name on the label instantly.

Zenoplyric acid.

The little glass vial was barely bigger than my finger. It was hard to believe that something so small could be the key to finding my parents.

All of a sudden, the alarm stopped. The sound of the

siren was replaced a second later by the crackle of a saw buzzing a hole into the barricaded doorway.

Someone was breaking into the room.

Whoever it was, it sounded like they were using a serious power tool to get through the door. I glanced back at the cloudy blue vial with a new sense of urgency. As carefully as possible, I removed it from the rack. Holding it out far in front of me, I turned it sideways to check the seal. If the stuff was as deadly as my parents had claimed, I didn't want it dripping down my leg. When I was sure the cap was secure, I cautiously placed the vial in my pants pocket.

I had just enough time to shove the doors of the cabinet closed before a massive chunk of the steel barrier fell onto the ground. I waited a moment more, my heart racing.

And then Captain Justice stepped into the room.

"Worry not, frightened child! Captain Justice is here to rescue you!"

He'd changed out of his exercise clothes and back into his usual uniform. His shining blue cape billowed behind him as he swept across the room toward me, muscles bulging beneath his silver jumpsuit.

I did my best to act natural, which meant pretending that there *wasn't* a glass vial of deadly acid in the pocket of my blue jeans.

"Sophie and Marlon are safely waiting outside until

the area is cleared of all dangers," Captain Justice said. He knelt down to my level. "Were you injured in any way during this traumatic ordeal?"

"Uh . . . I think I'll be okay."

"Excellent! In that case, let us make a quick and orderly exit from this—"

Captain Justice paused. His eyes flickered down to my pocket.

"What've you got there, son?"

I took a step back. "Huh?"

"In your pocket? What is that?"

A sinking feeling came over me. The acid. He must've noticed it. After coming all this way, I was so close. And now all of it was going to fall apart.

Captain Justice's expression sharpened. "Is there something you want to tell me?"

"No," I said. "Really, it's nothing."

He raised one eyebrow. "It doesn't *look* like nothing."

I tried to think of what to do, but every idea was worse than the previous one. Outrun Captain Justice? *Impossible.* Tell him I hadn't noticed the vial of deadly acid in my pocket? *Highly unlikely.*

Face it. The situation was hopeless.

"I'm sorry." My voice cracked. "I just—"

"No need to apologize," Captain Justice interrupted. "I know Justice Jerky when I see it."

For a moment, I thought my brain had missed a beat.

Then I glanced down. An empty wrapper of Justice Jerky was sticking out of my pocket.

"Er—that's right." My shoulders sank with relief. "I just can't get enough . . . Justice Jerky."

"And who can blame you!" A grin splashed across Captain Justice's face. "Justice Jerky combines rich beefy flavor with a spicy kick that will have you coming back for more every time!"

It was amazing. He sounded just like the commercials I'd seen a hundred times before.

"Now let's get you back to safety," Captain Justice said.

The parking lot was a madhouse. Flashing lights from ambulances and police cruisers cut through the darkness. The employees and security guards had been untied and were giving their statements to police officers and reporters. Several news vans were scattered nearby, a jumble of satellite dishes poking toward the sky.

As soon as we stepped outside, Captain Justice and I were surrounded by reporters. I felt an immediate rush of blood to my head at the sight of so many microphones and TV cameras coming my way, but Captain Justice handled himself much more naturally. Puffing out his chest, he held his chin up.

"Everything is under control." His voice boomed over the noisy parking lot. "The Dread Duo is nowhere to be found, and the missing children are all accounted for. Another evil scheme thwarted by Captain Justice."

I forgot about the reporters and the TV cameras, the police, and the chemical in my pocket. I replayed Captain Justice's words in my mind. *Another evil scheme thwarted by Captain Justice.* But he hadn't done anything to stop my parents. That had all been the work of the smoke creatures.

I glanced up at him, standing tall beside me. The spinning police lights flashed over his face, making his familiar features look strange and new.

While Captain Justice answered more of the journalists' questions, I ducked into the crowd in search of Milton and Sophie. I spotted them beside an ambulance.

"You're okay!" Sophie called out, rushing forward to hug me. "When those alarms started going off, I thought maybe something had happened. And then we couldn't find you, and—"

She seemed to realize that she had her arms around me about the same time I did. She let go instantly and we both took a step backward.

"Anyway, I'm glad you're okay," Sophie said.

"What took you so long?" Milton asked.

"I got a little delayed," I said. "But I also found something I wanted to show you. Just not here."

We headed off to the edge of the parking lot. When we

were far enough away from the crowd, I pulled the vial of cloudy blue liquid out of my pocket.

"The plenoryzic acid!" Milton exclaimed.

"*Zenoplyric,*" I corrected. "But yeah. I found it. Now we just need to get back to my house so we can track where my parents were transported."

"You're not thinking about going after them, are you?" Sophie asked.

"Of course I am! They're my parents!"

"I know, but—whoever's behind all this is dangerous. Maybe we should just tell the police—"

"Tell them *what*? That I need to track down my super-villain parents? If anything, the police will be happy they're gone. And they'll probably arrest me for stealing the chemical!"

"Well, then . . ." Sophie glanced off toward Captain Justice, who was still holding his press conference. "What about my dad?"

I snorted. "Oh, right. I'm sure he'd be thrilled to help us find his sworn enemies."

"Yeah, but . . . at least he has experience in this kind of thing."

I shook my head. There was another reason why I didn't want to tell Captain Justice. Just a feeling I had. It had started back in Sophie's house earlier in the day. The conversation between Captain Justice and the holographic head, the secret project only they knew about.

And just a few minutes ago—the way he'd said that *he'd* been the one who'd thwarted the Dread Duo even though the smoke creatures had been responsible for the attack.

I turned to Sophie and Milton, realization flooding through my mind. When I spoke, my voice was barely more than a whisper.

"Sophie, your dad?" I said. "I—I think he's the one who's controlling the smoke creatures."

20

**The difference between good and evil
isn't always as big as it seems.**

Sophie gasped. But it all made sense. The one thing that Captain Justice had in common with the smoke creatures was that they were both trying to rid the world of supervillains.

All this time, Captain Justice had been the one behind the plot to abduct supervillains.

Trying to convince Sophie and Milton of this wasn't so easy, though. Milton shook his head in disbelief. "No way," he said. "Captain Justice fights villains *himself.* He doesn't let some kind of smoke monsters do his work for him."

"That was before he started this secret new strategy," I explained.

Milton gave me a puzzled look. "What secret new strategy?"

"Earlier today, I overheard him during a holographic conference—"

"Wait a second," Sophie said. "You were eavesdropping on my dad?"

"No, I— It was an accident."

Sophie obviously didn't buy this excuse. She stared at me like she'd just noticed a disgusting new wart on my face.

"That's why you wanted to get that book," she said. "So you'd have a chance to sneak around my house. Were you spying for your parents? Trying to find inside information that would help them beat Captain Justice?"

"Of course not! I would never do that! I mean, sure . . . I was a little curious, but—"

Sophie let out a disbelieving laugh, crossing her arms.

"Look, the point is, he was talking about a secret project," I said. "Some kind of aggressive new strategy. He must've meant the smoke creatures, abducting supervillains . . ."

"But . . ." Milton knitted his brow. "It just doesn't sound like him."

"What about that article you showed me in *Super Scoop*? The shipment of robot parts to Sheepsdale?"

"So?"

"So the parts must've been going to Captain Justice. For the nano-beings."

Milton glanced back toward the other end of the parking lot. Captain Justice was signing autographs for the crowd.

"I guess I can kind of understand why he'd be doing it," he said. "I mean, he *is* still capturing bad guys. It's just a different way of doing it."

"Exactly," I said.

But Sophie wasn't so easily swayed. She kept her arms folded, staring at me like she was angry that I'd even suggested it was her dad.

"It can't be him," she insisted. "What about the Fire-bottomed Rompers? Whoever was controlling those things was also connected to the smoke creatures, right? And in case you forgot, I was there when they attacked us."

"Maybe he didn't know you'd be with me?" I said. "I'm the one with supervillains for parents. He must've assumed I'd be alone."

"Since when does my dad attack a supervillain's family? Anyway, he wouldn't have robots doing his work for him."

"What about Stanley? You have a robot driving

you around town. Why not use robots to capture villains too?"

"That's not the same thing, and you know it!"

Sophie looked like she wasn't ready to give up the argument yet, but she stopped talking abruptly when she noticed her hands. They were starting to glow. And so was the rest of her body. Her Gyft was shining through her like a mood ring she couldn't take off. Judging by the way she was glaring at me, I had the feeling her mood right then was somewhere between wanting to run away in embarrassment and wishing she could snap me in two. Instead, she took several deep breaths, waiting until the glow gradually faded.

"If you want to accuse my dad of something he isn't doing, that's fine," she said in a harsh whisper. "But don't expect me to go along with it."

Sophie stared at me for a second more, a faint glow still clinging to the edges of her eyes, and then she turned and stomped away.

Stanley was waiting nearby in the SUV. They didn't even drive past to say goodbye before leaving Milton and me in the parking lot, without a ride home. I could understand why she might have been upset. I'd just accused her dad of abducting my parents and trying to kill the three of us. But that didn't change the way I felt about Captain Justice. I was certain he was the one behind the smoke creatures. And I intended to find out where he'd transported my parents.

Milton called his mom, and she came to pick us up. It wasn't so easy to explain why we were spending our Friday night surrounded by police cars and news vans outside a building that had been attacked by supervillains a couple of hours earlier.

"We . . . uh . . . asked to be dropped off when we saw Captain Justice outside that building," Milton said. "You know, to see if we could get his autograph."

Luckily, Milton's mom was just as big a fan of Captain Justice's as Milton was. And he even had the autographed copy of *Super Scoop* from earlier. When he showed it to her, Milton's mom squealed like a teenage girl and nearly swerved off the road.

After that, Milton had no problem convincing her to let me spend the night at his house. Which was a good thing, since I definitely wasn't looking forward to sleeping in my house now that my parents were gone.

Milton's mom dropped me off at my house so I could pick up my stuff for the night. Then I'd walk over to their house. As the sound of their car receded down the street, I crossed the lawn alone. At the front door, I unlocked three deadbolts, punched in the security code, deactivated the alarm sensors, and pressed my thumb against a pad to authenticate my identity.

Then I stepped inside.

The house felt different somehow. As if my parents' absence had already seeped into the furniture and the walls. Micus must've known something was wrong, because he didn't threaten to kill me once while I passed through the dining room. He just stayed in his usual spot in the corner, his branches slumped forward sadly.

My feet clumped hollowly against the steps as I made my way up the stairs. After entering my parents' lab, I removed the vial of acid from my pocket and approached the glass case. It still looked empty, but I knew that somewhere inside was the nano-being.

I noticed something different about the computer next to the case, though. It was covered in labels. Little yellow slips stuck here and there. One of them read, *Insert chemical compound here*, with an arrow pointing to a slot in the machine. My eyes passed over another: *Press this button to activate tracking sequence*.

Gradually it dawned on me. My parents hadn't made these labels for their own use. They'd made them for me.

They must've known there was a chance they'd be attacked before they could get the chemical. That was why they'd brought me up here to explain exactly what the smoke creatures were and how to trace them. That was why they'd carefully labeled every step needed to run the tracking sequence.

They wanted me to know how to find them if they went missing.

I placed the vial into the slot and lowered a long straw into the liquid. Following the instructions my parents had left behind, I turned on the computer terminal and pressed another button that caused a single droplet of acid to rise up the straw and into a hole in the glass case. I took a deep breath and initiated the tracking sequence.

I stared at the monitor. At first, nothing happened. But after several seconds, a box popped up on the screen.

Coordinate Tracking Results
Lat: +45.262321
Lon: -69.012489

In geography the previous year, we'd spent an entire class pushing pins into a wall map where the lines of latitude and longitude met. "Lat" must have been short for "latitude." Which meant that "Lon" was an abbreviation for "longitude."

I typed "latitude longitude" into Google. After selecting the first site that showed up, I entered the numbers into the coordinate tracking boxes. Latitude: +45.262321, longitude: -69.012489. An instant later, a location appeared on the screen.

Carrolshire, Maine.

I printed out the map and the coordinates, grabbed my toothbrush and a clean T-shirt, and then headed to Milton's.

After breakfast the next morning, Milton and I stepped out onto his front doorstep. A familiar black SUV had parked along the curb outside my house. A moment later, the door opened and Sophie climbed out.

"What're you doing here?" I asked, running to meet her.

"I thought maybe you could use some help," she said.

"But what about last night?"

Sophie stared down at her shadow, which stretched across the grass. "Maybe I overreacted just a little bit. And . . . well—there's something else. Last night, after I went home, I found *this*."

She reached into the SUV, removed something, and held it out so that only Milton and I could see. A thick silver wristband, the kind Captain Justice wore to create all his holo-weapons.

"It's a brand-new model," Sophie said. "I've never seen him wearing it before. I found it inside a box marked 'confidential.'"

Sophie flipped the wristband over and showed us what was printed on the underside.

Multifunction Utility Band™

A chill gripped my heart. The last time I'd seen that Z logo, I'd been running for my life, trying to avoid getting killed by a horde of Firebottomed Rompers.

"He had at least fifty other boxes," Sophie said. "Uniforms, accessories, capes. All of them with this logo on there somewhere."

"So it really *was* him?" Milton sounded like it hurt just to say these words. "Your dad is the one behind the smoke creatures and the Rompers?"

Sophie nodded, her expression hardening. "It has to be. I can't see any other explanation."

"Did you ask him about it?"

"I didn't get a chance. He left before I woke up this morning. Stanley said he had to go to some town in Maine."

"Carrolshire?" I asked.

Sophie gave me a surprised look. "How'd you know?"

"Because I'm pretty sure that's where my parents are."

I pulled the map with the coordinates out of my pocket and told her what I'd discovered the night before.

"We need to find a way to get to Carrolshire," Sophie said.

"Does that mean you're coming too?" I asked.

"Of course. If my dad's really doing this, I want to be the one to call him out on it."

"This is awesome!" Milton said. "I mean, not the part about your parents disappearing or your dad trying to kill us. But the three of us going on an adventure—it's like we're superheroes!"

I turned to face him. "What do you mean 'the *three* of us'?"

Milton clenched his jaw. "I'm coming too."

"You can't," I said. "It could be dangerous. And you're not . . . I mean—you don't have any . . ."

"Powers?" Milton jammed his hands into his pockets. "I can't go because I'm not *special* like the two of you—is that what you're saying?"

"Kind of. You could get really hurt."

But Milton wasn't giving in. He stomped the pavement with one foot, looking at me with pleading in his eyes. "I thought we were best friends."

"We are—"

"And best friends help each other out, right?"

"Yeah, but—"

"Remember that time you had that weird rash on your armpit and I didn't tell anyone?"

"Thanks for the reminder," I muttered. "What's your point?"

"I was there for you!" Milton said. "Just like that time you let your hair grow long and everyone started mistaking you for a girl? I supported you then too. And that time when—"

"Fine," I said, before Milton could get any more out. "You can come too."

"Great!" Milton pumped his fist with excitement. "How are we gonna get to Maine?"

I glanced at Sophie. "Could Stanley drive us?"

Sophie shook her head. "He isn't allowed to drive me outside the county limit without my dad's authorization. He's been programmed that way."

"And my mom is hosting her book club today," Milton said. "So she can't."

"What about the bus?" Sophie asked.

"I already checked that," I said. "There aren't any stops near Carrolshire."

"So, then, what are we gonna do?" Milton asked.

I looked past Milton, my eyes landing on my closed garage door. And that's when it hit me.

"Milton, it's your lucky day," I said.

21

Hover vehicles are subject to intense government regulation. They also get horrible gas mileage. You should use them only when it's absolutely necessary.

My parents kept their hover scooters in the corner of the garage. Even after Mom's scooter had been blasted to smithereens during their attempt to flood the earth, they still had three older models that we could use. Luckily, I'd played around on their scooters enough over the years to know how to operate them.

With my feet planted against the metal board at the bottom, I flipped the On/Off switch. The hover scooter shivered as the engine began to hum. I gripped the handles and pulled upward very gently. The scooter lifted off the ground. Leaning forward on the handlebar caused the scooter to float forward. Pulling it backward put it into reverse.

After giving a few more tips to Sophie and Milton, we found bike helmets and began to practice in the backyard.

Sophie figured it out right away. Within minutes, she was hovering across the yard. Soon she was accelerating her scooter from one side of the yard to the other.

Milton took a little longer.

"Make sure you pull up *gently*," I said.

"Gently," Milton said. "Got it."

Milton concentrated on the handlebars.

"Is it doing anything?" he asked.

"Not yet."

"What about now? Am I flying?"

"No, you're still on the ground."

"Are you sure?"

"Maybe you're being a little *too* gentle. Try pulling up a bit harder."

Milton yanked upward on the handle. All of a sudden, the scooter burst fifty feet into the air. He screamed, hugging the handlebars close to his chest as he shot into the sky like a Milton-sized bottle rocket.

"Too hard!" I called up to him.

"You think so?" he screamed. "How do I get down?"

"Just push down on the handle—very softly. And be careful that you don't—"

Before I could finish, the scooter performed several front flips. It would've actually been a kind of impressive maneuver if he hadn't been screaming in a high-pitched wail the entire time.

"Milton!" I called. "Be careful not to twist the handles."

But by this time, he'd lost control completely. A few seconds later, he was circling the yard upside down, hanging from the handlebars. He twisted and spun in the air, narrowly avoiding the roof. He finally came to a stop when he got snagged in the branches of a tree.

After a few more practice rounds, Milton got the hang of it. He hopped from foot to foot, gazing at his scooter proudly. "It's like a real adventure! And you know what every good adventure needs, right?"

I shook my head.

"Snacks! If you let me borrow your backpack, I'll get everything we need."

"Fine." I went inside and grabbed my backpack. As I handed it over to Milton, I reminded him, "Just essential items."

Milton came back a few minutes later. The backpack was stuffed full of Dr Pepper, potato chips, and Justice Jerky.

I entered the coordinates into the VexaCorp navigator that was built into the front panel display of my scooter. A map showed up on the LCD screen, displaying the route to Carrolshire.

"Ready?" I said, glancing at Sophie and Milton.

"Ready," they said at the same time.

We boarded our scooters and launched into the air.

If you've never traveled long distance by hover scooter before, I recommend it. The wind blasted my face as the landscape of country roads and fields drifted beneath us. I swallowed a few bugs along the way, but otherwise it was great.

After we'd been in the air for a few hours, the GPS system showed us nearing our destination. Up ahead I spotted the shape of a lone building on the horizon.

"I think that's where we're headed," I called out.

"Looks like we're not the only ones in the air." Milton pointed at a cluster of birds flying above the building. There were at least a dozen of them, circling the building in a tight formation. As if they were guarding the place.

My grip tightened on the scooter's handlebars. The birds were about the size of crows, but they didn't look like any crows I'd ever seen. Their beaks and legs were silver. They had jet-black bodies that reflected the sunlight as they cut through the air.

As we got closer, the birds stopped patrolling the air around the building and instead began flying in our direction.

"I've got a bad feeling about this!" I yelled.

"M-maybe they're just migrating south for the winter," Milton said. But I could tell from his shaking voice that he didn't believe it.

"We're too vulnerable up here," Sophie called. "We need to get onto solid ground."

We steered our scooters downward, bringing them to rest on a vacant field. I was still holding on to a scrap of hope that the birds would pass over us. But by the looks of it, they had other plans. I squinted into the sky, fear darkening my thoughts. The birds were descending on us like fighter jets.

Their shadows surrounded us. A split second later, the birds were everywhere.

Sophie, Milton, and I went running in different directions, trailed closely by swarms of birds. Shielding my face with one arm, I swung with the other, making contact with a bird that was trying to dive-bomb my head—

CLANG!

Pain erupted in my hand. It felt like I'd just slammed my knuckles against a steel pipe. Their beaks were silver and sharp as daggers. Their bodies were covered in smooth, black metal. I could hear the electronic whir of their wings.

These weren't birds. They were machines.

"Why do robots seem to attack me every time I hang

out with you guys?" Milton screamed, ducking out of the way of a kamikaze bird.

A metallic *clack* rang out as I knocked another bird into the dirt. But there were plenty more where that had come from, flapping around me from all sides. If it hadn't been for my bike helmet, my head would've looked like Swiss cheese.

Focus! I told myself—not the easiest thing to do when a flock of mechanical crows was trying to peck my eyes out. I thought back on all the practice I'd had over the last few weeks—setting twigs on fire and heating up snacks after school. This wasn't all that different, right? *Just think of the birds like big Hot Pockets with wings.* Hot Pockets that were trying to eat me instead of the other way around.

I swung my arm, and a surge of energy pulsed through my veins. The birds were consumed in an explosion that knocked me onto my back. A wave of heat pushed past me. And a smell. The smell of short-circuited wires.

The charred remains of robot birds were scattered around me. Dismantled wings and wires, broken legs still twitching.

Nearby, Sophie was back in full glowing mode. She ripped one bird out of the air and chopped another in half with the side of her hand. A third was dismantled with a single kick.

"Guys!" Milton screamed from behind us. "A little help!"

Shiny metallic birds flapped all around him. He struck out at one, spun around, and then lost his balance and fell to the ground. The birds swept down on him in an instant.

Sophie was already running. When she reached Milton, she punched one of the birds into oblivion. Scrap metal flew everywhere. She chopped a second bird to the ground just as I arrived.

I grabbed a bird out of the air just before it could plunge its silver beak into Milton's throat. Another throb of energy passed through me, and the thing exploded into a thousand pieces.

Once we'd finished off the last of the birds, an eerie silence settled over the field. The sounds of clanking metal and flapping mechanical wings were suddenly gone. Now I could only hear my own heavy breathing.

Milton rose onto one elbow, brushing pieces of grass and bird parts off his clothes. "These robots really hate you guys, huh?"

"I guess you could say that." Sophie picked up a part of one of the birds—a midsection with only one wing attached to it. A familiar logo was etched into the smooth, black surface.

Z

Guard Bird™

"What do you think they were guarding?" I asked.

"I don't know." Milton shrugged. "But whatever it is, it's inside there."

He cast a nervous glance toward the building in the distance. It was a grim old structure that looked like it had been abandoned years ago. Tangled vines clung to the gray walls; boards were nailed across the windows.

Leaving our hover scooters in the tall grass, we approached the building. Getting closer, I spotted a faded sign outside that read:

OCEAN VIEW HOT L

"What kind of a name is that?" Milton asked. "I don't even see any ocean."

"And there isn't much of a view either," I added, surveying the dreary fields all around.

The only sign that anyone had visited the hotel in the past decade was the brand-new red convertible parked in the overgrown dirt road out front. The license plate read:

JUSTICE

Turning to Sophie, I saw that she was still holding the bird fragment in one hand. Her eyes moved from the car to the *Z* logo engraved into the bird's midsection.

"How could my dad be doing this?" she whispered.

I didn't know how to respond, and I doubted Sophie was waiting for an answer anyway. She threw the bird at the ground with so much force that the remaining wing broke off. Then she stomped up the shaky steps leading to the front door of the hotel. When she turned the rusted knob, the door creaked open.

Hesitating on the doorstep, the three of us peered into the dark interior. Then we stepped inside.

22

You can't always rely on your Gyft alone. Sometimes you'll need skill, talent— and luck.

The inside of the hotel was even crummier than the outside.

Near the front door, a stairway twisted upward into the shadows. At the bottom of the stairs, two rusty iron gargoyles leered in our general direction. Dreary curtains covered the lobby windows. Everything was shrouded in darkness. There was no sign of Captain Justice, or anyone else.

We were alone.

The floorboards groaned beneath our feet as we

passed a long reception desk. But like everything else, it was vacant.

At the far end of the lobby was an open corridor. Out of the corner of my eye, I thought I noticed a dark shape moving across the open space. But when I looked, there was nothing except faded carpeting and peeling wallpaper.

"Are you sure we should be here?" Milton asked. "Maybe there's a bed-and-breakfast somewhere nearby that we should check first."

"My dad's here," Sophie said. "We just need to find him."

We pushed open a door that led into a vast room with dirty tiled walls. In the center of the room, the floor dropped away, revealing an empty pit. The hollow space was surrounded by plastic lounge chairs.

"It's the indoor swimming pool," Sophie said. "They drained out all the water."

There may not have been any water, but the pool wasn't empty. At the bottom was a pile of supervillain uniforms and accessories. I recognized the cape and spear that had once belonged to the Abominator. The big armor-plated gloves of Tesla the Terrible.

And then my heart clenched as I noticed a pair of my dad's customized goggles at the top of the heap. Nearby was a green and black bundle of spandex and body armor that could only be my mom's.

"My parents," I whispered. "They're here. Or at least, they *were*."

I stared down into the drained pool. A shadow shifted across my thoughts.

"Why is all this stuff just piled in here like this?" I asked. "You don't think my parents have been—"

"No," Sophie said. She must've known what I'd been about to say. "My dad wouldn't do that."

"What about the smoke creatures and the Fire-bottomed Rompers your dad's controlling?" I said. "What about all the other secrets your dad's keeping from you?"

Sophie shot an angry glance my way. But I felt too full of fear and anger to keep my mouth shut.

"Maybe your dad isn't who you think he is," I said.

Sophie's hands were curled into trembling fists.

"Hey, come on," Milton said in a fake cheerful tone. "We don't know what happened here. I'm sure your parents are fine." He patted me on the back. "They probably just took off their clothes so they could go skinny-dipping."

The thought of a hundred supervillains skinny-dipping together didn't cheer me up (especially since my parents were part of the group). Besides, this didn't look like the kind of place that had a Jacuzzi. There had to be another explanation for why all these clothes had been dumped here. And I knew it wasn't good.

"Come on," I said. "We might not have much time."

We'd nearly reached the other end of the pool when a dark form shifted out of the shadows. A jolt of fear shot through my chest. The figure turned to gaze at us, but where its face should've been, there was only a featureless cloud.

A smoke creature.

It was standing in the corner, right next to a NO LIFEGUARD ON DUTY sign.

I spun around to run in the direction we'd come from, but that was as far as I got. A second smoke creature was headed toward us.

"This way!" Sophie pointed to the door at the other end of the room.

Our footsteps echoed off the tiled walls as we raced along the edge of the pool, past a rack of foam noodles and kickboards that looked like they'd last been played with before I was born. The smoke creatures stalked toward us, getting steadily closer.

One of them reached out, its fingers like tendrils of smoke. I kept running, following Sophie and Milton through a narrow hallway that wove in and out of crumbling rooms and empty offices.

The dilapidated scenery of the hotel blurred all around me. Broken furniture, dusty antiques, tilted chandeliers. There was no time to figure out where we were going. The smoke creatures were trailing close behind, their dark bodies moving soundlessly in our wake.

We turned down a corridor that led into a kitchen, and ran past a refrigerator with a missing door, and a broken-down stove. Milton collided with a counter, sending a cascade of rusted pots and pans crashing to the ground.

Bursting through the door, we found ourselves in a ballroom. Like the rest of the hotel, it looked like the ruins of a place that might've been nice many years ago. Faded velvet curtains lined the walls. The bar in the corner looked like it had been hit by a wrecking ball.

The smoke creatures swept into the room a few seconds after us. We started toward the other end of the ballroom, but came to a halt when we saw what had just emerged from the opposite doors. Another pair of smoke creatures. There were four of them now, blocking both the exits.

We were surrounded.

"What do we do now?" Milton was staring at the approaching smoke creatures, his eyes wide with fear.

"I don't know," I said, "but we've got to think of something. Just don't panic."

"Too late!"

The cloudy figures were closing in on us, their smoke legs carrying them swiftly across the stained carpets.

I looked around the ramshackle ballroom, searching desperately for some kind of an escape. Then I caught .

sight of a boarded-up fireplace near the bar. If we could get there in time, maybe we could climb to safety.

Sophie had the same idea. She took off running toward the fireplace, and Milton and I trailed close behind. By the time she got there, the glow was radiating from her skin. She ripped the boards away like they were made of paper.

"Whoa," she said, peering into the fireplace.

Looking over her shoulder, I saw what had caught her attention. This wasn't an ordinary fireplace. It was a tunnel.

There wasn't any time to wonder why this hotel came with a walk-in fireplace or where the tunnel led. Smoke creatures were steadily drifting toward us.

"Get inside, quick!" My voice echoed in the tunnel.

Milton was first, followed by Sophie. The smoke creatures were looming over me as I scrambled in after her.

The narrow passageway slanted steeply downward, curving so that it seemed as if we were burrowing deeper and deeper into the earth. It was dark, but fortunately Sophie was glowing like a human night-light, illuminating the stone tunnel that seemed to go on without end.

My shoes slipped over the steep rocky floor, and my arms scraped against the jagged walls, but there was no way I was slowing down.

I let out a sharp gasp when I felt something grab hold of my ankle. Falling forward suddenly, terror shot through me. Lurching sideways, I expected to see the dark shapes of smoke creatures swooping down. But the tunnel behind me was empty. No smoke creatures. Nothing.

My ankle was wedged into a hole in the ground.

I took a deep breath to calm myself, then yanked my foot free. Peering back the way we'd come, I could see the cloudy silhouettes of the smoke creatures in the mouth of the fireplace we'd entered through.

"Looks like we're not being followed anymore," I said.

"Why do you think they stopped?" Sophie asked.

"Maybe smoke monsters are claustrophobic." Milton's shaky voice echoed. "Or maybe there's something at the end of this tunnel that even *they* would rather avoid."

"Well, unless we want to go back and ask them personally, our only choice is to keep going," Sophie said.

We continued downward, trudging at a slower pace now that we knew we weren't being pursued. I watched the shadows bouncing off the stone walls, and listened to the sound of our footsteps echoing dully in the passageway.

Eventually we saw a pale light shining up ahead. The tunnel leveled out. We kept walking, trying to create as little noise as possible. Sophie's Gyft must've been winding down, because her glow was fading. By the time we reached the end of the tunnel, her skin looked normal again.

Ahead of us was an opening. Milton passed though it first, then Sophie, then me. As I emerged, I caught my breath.

In front of us was a steel platform. Beyond that was a cavernous room that stretched far beneath us. A stairway to our left led to the bottom of the chamber. If the rest of the hotel had seemed like it had been rotting away for the last fifty years, this room looked like something from the future.

The platform was lined by two-story silver canisters. Wires protruded from the bottoms of the canisters like tangles of unmoving snakes.

"I can't believe all this is connected to that old hotel," I whispered.

Taking cover, we gazed down at the room beneath us. More silver canisters lined the walls, each of them connected to dozens of wires that all led in the same direction—toward a wall of glass. I strained to see what was behind the glass, but it was too dark.

A movement caught my eye, and all at once I knew we weren't alone. Two men were walking toward the center of the room. One of them had a dark suit and a face that seemed weirdly familiar.

The other man was much easier to recognize. There was no mistaking the silver uniform, the shimmering blue cape and matching gloves.

"Dad?" Sophie said.

At the sound of her voice, Captain Justice and the other man spun around.

Milton and I kept ourselves hidden behind one of the huge canisters while Sophie descended the stairs.

"Sophie?" Captain Justice said. "What the blazes are you doing here?"

"I was going to ask you the same thing," she said.

"How did you know where I was? How did you even *get* here? Did Stanley drive you? I'm going to have to reprogram that robot as soon as I—"

"Stanley didn't drive me. I found another way to get here."

"What's going on, Captain J?" asked the man in the suit.

As soon as he spoke, I realized where I'd seen him before. He was the hologram head. Fink.

Sophie's feet clanged against each metal step until she reached the bottom of the stairs.

"I know you're a family man and everything," Fink said to Captain Justice, "but I thought this was a private meeting."

"It is," Captain Justice said. "Sophie, you shouldn't be here."

"I already know about your secret project," Sophie countered.

Captain Justice's forehead wrinkled with confusion. "You *do*? But . . . how?"

"It doesn't matter. The point is, I know—and I came here to ask you to stop."

"Look, darling . . . I am aware that this might seem like a big change, but sometimes change is necessary."

"Why are you being so secretive about it, then?"

"I was going to make an announcement. That's why Fink and I are meeting. We're here to discuss the next stage of the project. The press release is already written, the new uniform has been designed—"

"Okay, I think we've all gotten a little ahead of ourselves," Fink interrupted. "Maybe it's best if we talk about this later—"

But Sophie ignored Fink. "I know all about it, Dad," she said. "Your little scheme to have microscopic robots teleport all the supervillains in the world."

"Microscopic robots? Teleport?" Captain Justice shook his head.

"Captain J," said Fink, "I really think that we should—"

"You nearly killed me and my friends—twice!" Sophie said. "Is that a part of your plan too?"

"Sophie, I would never . . ." Captain Justice looked bewildered, as if he were hearing about the details of his plan for the first time. "You must be mistaken. Fink and I are working on a secret project, that's true. But it has nothing to do with teleporting villains or trying to kill anyone."

Before Captain Justice could say anything more, Fink reached into his pocket and removed a cell phone. He jabbed a finger at the touch pad. An instant later, an enormous glowing red wall formed around where Sophie and Captain Justice were standing, trapping them in place like a cage. Fink stared back at them from the other side of the barrier, the cell phone clutched in one hand.

Captain Justice beat his fists against the glowing wall. But no matter how hard he pounded, the barrier stayed in place.

"What is this, Fink?" Captain Justice yelled. "What have you done?"

"I'm sorry, Captain J," Fink said from the other side of the barrier, "but like you said, sometimes change is necessary."

"Curse you, Fink! Let us out of this thing at once!"

"I'm afraid I can't do that. My boss wants to keep you there."

"I *am* your boss!"

"Not anymore. I have a new boss now. And he pays considerably more."

There was a sound at the other end of the room.

Footsteps. The rhythm of shoes moving across the floor. And something else—the steady click of a cane.

A figure emerged from the shadows. A man shrouded in darkness. He moved slowly, supporting himself with his cane as he approached the glowing barrier.

Phineas Vex.

23

**The Handbook for Gyfted Children
is a resource that will be useful to you
in many different ways.**

I thought about the last time I'd seen Phineas Vex—
struggling in the grip of a smoke creature, just before he'd disappeared in a burst of lightning. Milton and I watched, hidden behind the canister, as he neared the glowing barrier where Sophie and Captain Justice were trapped.

"Greetings, Captain Justice," Phineas Vex said.

He spoke in the same commanding voice that I remembered from the Vile Fair. A black patch covered one eye. A scar ran down the side of his face.

"Release me at once!" Captain Justice hollered at Vex.

"Release you?" Vex let out a single barking laugh. "After all the work I put into getting you here? I don't think so."

"Very well," Captain Justice said. "I'll just have to release myself."

Vex watched, amused, as Captain Justice held out his arm, pointing his fist at the glowing boundary.

"Engage Heat Beam of Honesty!" he bellowed. Nothing happened. He pressed a button on his armor-plated wristband and tried again.

"I'm afraid your arsenal of badly named hologram weapons won't work," said Vex. "Nor will any other powers. The barrier emits an energy field that neutralizes all superpowers and disables any electronic devices. You can't even get a cell phone signal in there."

Vex turned to Sophie.

"You must be Sophie Justice," he said, bending forward and leaning on his cane with both gloved hands. "You look just like your mother."

A twisted smile formed on his scarred face.

Sophie stepped forward. Captain Justice tried to pull her back, but she stood her ground, staring at Vex through the glowing barrier.

"I must say I'm impressed that you survived this long," Vex said. "Especially after my attempt to"—his awful smile sharpened—"send you a message."

"The Firebottomed Rompers?" Sophie said.

"That's right. When I discovered that Captain Justice had moved to Sheepsdale, I decided to send his daughter a welcoming committee. Unfortunately, you and your little friends survived. And I suppose you must've made it past my flock of Guard Birds as well."

"And the smoke creatures," Sophie said.

"In that case, you at least deserve to know that your father is telling the truth about his secret project. It has nothing to do with teleporting villains. It's more of a . . . How would you describe it, Fink?"

"A rebranding effort," Fink said.

"That's right," Vex said. "Rebranding."

Sophie turned to Captain Justice. "Is that true, Dad?"

Captain Justice nodded. "The brand was going stale. We were losing several key demographics. Our plan was to update my image. New uniform, new accessories. Even a new name." He paused for effect. "Captain Justiz—with a z."

"So that's why you had all that stuff with the Z logo on it," Sophie said. "But what about the smoke creatures?"

"That was my contribution," Vex replied. "VexaCorp developed the nano-beings for the smoke creatures. And the smoke creatures brought the villains to me."

Fink reached into his pocket and retrieved his cell phone. The same phone he'd used to generate the neutralizing barrier around Sophie and Captain Justice.

This time when he punched a button, a light flickered on behind the glass.

There were people back there—more than a hundred of them. Villains. They were all dressed in identical white robes, and they were being held to the wall by thick metal restraints. Their bodies were slumped forward, their eyes closed.

My mom and dad were near the far end of the glass. Like everyone else, they were draped in white robes. Their wrists and legs were secured to the wall. Their heads drooped toward the ground.

"The world's most dangerous supervillains," Vex said with a note of awe in his voice. "All here in one room. They're in artificially induced comas right now. They'll stay that way until I release them."

"You're insane," Captain Justice said. "These are *your* customers. Why would you abduct them?"

"Oh, but you're wrong there." A malicious grin formed on Vex's face. "I didn't abduct these villains. *You* did."

A pause filled the room. Captain Justice took a step away from the glowing wall that separated him from Vex.

"What are you talking about?" he asked.

"On paper, all this is yours." Vex gestured toward the rows of massive computers, the machinery, the unconscious supervillains behind him. "Thanks to Fink here, everything connected to the disappearing villains leads right back to Captain Justice. Not to mention the smoke creatures and Firebottomed Rompers. The research and development budgets. Even this hotel. Everything is registered under Justiz Industries. And Justiz Industries is registered under *your* name."

Captain Justice stared back at Vex with a stunned expression. I'd seen him hundreds of times before—on magazines, in commercials, fighting my parents—but he'd never looked as confused as he did now.

"You still don't get it, do you?" Vex said. "I suppose that's to be expected. Intelligence was never your greatest strength. All along, you thought you and Fink were just working on some paltry little rebranding. *Captain Justiz.* But Fink was putting in a lot of extra hours without your knowledge to make sure that all of *this*"—Vex gestured to the underground chamber, the wall of unconscious villains—"is linked back to *you.*"

"You're even more demented than you look, Vex!" Captain Justice said. "Nobody will believe these lies!"

"Of course they will! You have the money; you have the motivation. The paperwork, the patents—they're all in your name. When investigators look into the smoke creatures, they'll find the *Z* logo imprinted on the sides of each nano-robot. The same logo that you have on all your new uniforms and accessories."

The wristband that Sophie had shown me that morning. *He had at least fifty other boxes,* she'd said.

PHINEAS VEX

The founder of VexaCorp Industries,
Phineas Vex is behind many of the most
popular (and deadly) supervillain products
on the market. If you see the eyes of his
skull cane begin to glow red, it could be
lights-out for you.

Uniforms, accessories, capes. All of them with this logo on there somewhere.

"Nobody will ever suspect I was involved," Vex said. "Why would they? An entire conference hall full of supervillains witnessed me being abducted by one of the smoke creatures when I courageously stepped in to rescue a boy at the Vile Fair."

"Even if you *do* succeed in this deception, the public will be grateful," Captain Justice said. "With so many supervillains in captivity, the world will be a safer place. And I'll be the one to get credit for it."

"That would be true. Except I intend to release the villains. Just as soon as I've finished killing you and your daughter."

A terrible silence hung over the room.

"Allow me to explain what all the newspapers will be reporting tomorrow morning, since you won't be alive to read any of them," Vex said coolly. "Captain Justice's secret plan to teleport supervillains fell apart when one of them—a certain Phineas Vex—managed to escape. Captain Justice tried to stop him and a battle ensued, but Vex got the upper hand, and Captain Justice—the greatest superhero the world has ever known—perished once and for all."

Captain Justice looked like he wanted to strangle Vex. But Vex went on, his single eye trained unblinkingly through the barrier.

"As soon as you and your daughter are out of the way, I'll free the rest of the supervillains that are trapped here. I'll tell them everything. How you were the one controlling the smoke creatures. About my escape, our fight. They've been in comas since arriving here. They'll believe all of it. And so will the media. Especially when they discover all the paperwork in your name. Once the story goes public, it will do more for my image—and the image of VexaCorp—than any amount of marketing money ever could have. The world will fear me. The supervillain community will worship me."

"Are you saying that this is all just a"—Captain Justice shook his head—"a public relations campaign?"

"Now you're catching on. You and I both know that *image* is everything in our line of work. Without it, heroes and villains are just a bunch of lunatics flying around in funny costumes." Vex laughed, a low, dark chuckle. "I will forever be known as the villain who killed Captain Justice and rescued the world's worst supervillains. Do you have any idea what this kind of publicity will do for the profit margin of VexaCorp?"

Vex tapped his cane once on the hard floor, like a punctuation mark to his wild story.

"You're crazy," Captain Justice said. But there was no trace of the booming confidence I'd always heard from him in the past. He sounded almost . . . afraid. "You'll never succeed."

209

"I already have," Vex replied. "You and your daughter will soon be dead. And Fink is the only other person who can contradict the story. But since he'll be dead soon too, I doubt he'll be giving any press conferences."

Fink spun to face Vex, his face transforming with surprise and fear. "What?" he muttered. "What are you—"

Before he could say anything more, Vex lifted his cane, aiming the skull handle at Fink's chest. A beam of red light shot out of the handle, and Fink collapsed onto the ground.

Captain Justice rushed forward. "You madman!" he screamed.

A sickening chill crept down my neck. The cane in Vex's hand—it had ended Fink's life in a single flash of red light.

Vex bent down and removed the phone from the pocket of Fink's jacket.

"Technology truly is a wonderful thing," he said, admiring the phone. "When I was first starting out in the supervillain business, we needed a computer the size of an ice cream truck just to power a graphing calculator. Now I can control every function of this lair with a smartphone. There's an app for everything. All I have to do is press this touch pad, and it will trigger a stream of poisonous gas inside the neutralizing barrier that will kill you both within minutes."

I'd been watching all this with a growing sense

of terror. Milton was beside me, his mouth hanging open like he'd just sat through a six-hour horror movie marathon.

"What do we do?" he whispered.

"I don't know." My voice was so quiet that I barely heard it myself. "But we can't just wait here for Vex to kill them."

As quietly as possible, Milton unzipped the backpack. "Maybe there's something in here we can use," he whispered, pulling out cans of Dr Pepper, bags of chips, packs of Justice Jerky.

Our lives were on the line, and the only weapon we had was junk food.

"Hey, what's this?" Milton took out *The Handbook for Gyfted Children*.

I hadn't even known it was in there when I'd let Milton borrow the backpack. Not that it would do us much good now. What was I supposed to do with a *book*? Unless there was a chapter I hadn't noticed entitled "How to Stop a Psycho Supervillain and His Killer Cane," it was worthless at a time like this.

Or maybe it wasn't. . . .

I grabbed hold of the book. Over the past couple of weeks, I'd read and reread all the parts that I'd hoped would help me figure out who I was. And now I could think of only one thing to do with it.

"No matter what happens," I whispered to Milton,

"just stay down. Make sure Vex doesn't see you. And keep away from his cane."

I took a deep breath, gripping the book tighter. And then I stood up.

The scene below flashed across my eyes in an instant. Sophie and Captain Justice huddled behind the glowing barrier. Vex a few feet away, the cell phone in one hand, the cane in the other.

Before I had a chance to lose my nerve, I took aim and threw *The Handbook for Gyfted Children* as hard as I could. All the built-up energy inside me crackled across my skin. The book burst into flames as soon as it left my hand. A trail of fire swept behind it like a comet.

Vex spun around just in time. He ducked, and the book went flying right into one of the massive silver canisters behind him.

KA-BOOOOM!

The canister exploded instantaneously, sending out a wave of heat that I felt from all the way across the vast room. The detonation knocked Vex to the ground. The phone flew out of his hand and skidded across the floor.

Behind the glowing barrier, Sophie and Captain Justice looked unharmed by the explosion. I couldn't say the same for Vex. He was lying on his stomach, his cane gripped loosely in one hand. He wasn't moving, but I could tell he was conscious by the look in his one good eye. It was focused on something several feet away.

The phone.

All at once, I knew what needed to be done. Vex had said that the phone controlled everything. If I could get to it before he did, I could save Sophie and Captain Justice—and release my parents while I was at it.

My footsteps clanged against metal as I sprinted across the platform. Below me, the flames were spreading. Another of the massive canisters exploded. The blast rocked the platform, and I tumbled headfirst onto metal grating.

Climbing to my feet, I saw Vex—standing on one knee, flames rising up behind him. He was gripping his skull cane, pointing it at my chest, just like he'd done right before Fink had dropped dead.

The eyes of the skull grew piercingly red. I felt a jolt. And then everything went dark.

24

Just because you're different doesn't mean you can't have a happy, normal childhood. But keep in mind: Gyfted kids are statistically more likely to find themselves in dangerous and life-threatening situations.

When I opened my eyes, I saw Milton staring down at me.

"Am I dead?" I mumbled.

"Nope." Milton shook his head. "You're in Maine."

My head dropped back. In the instant before Vex could zap me with his death cane, I'd caught a glimpse of Milton—running way faster than I'd ever seen him move in PE. As the red glow had burst out of the eyes of Vex's skull cane, Milton had knocked me out of the way. He'd saved my life.

I climbed to my knees. The platform rumbled underneath me with the force of another explosion. Vex was back on his feet now, staggering toward the phone.

I grabbed hold of a piece of metal debris and threw it at Vex. It shot through the air like a deadly flaming Frisbee. Vex aimed the handle of his cane, the skull's eyes glowing red, and the sheet of metal exploded. I dove out of the way to avoid the same thing happening to my head.

Time was running out. Vex was nearing the phone, and there was no way I'd get there in time to stop him. My eyes flashed over to the glowing barrier, where Sophie was hunched next to her dad. Fear clenched inside my chest. I wondered if this was the last time I'd ever see them alive.

Vex lunged for the phone just as another canister exploded. The blast sent him tumbling sideways. Flames flew everywhere, and the floor jolted again beneath me. The platform was about to collapse.

Milton and I grabbed hold of the railing, but it didn't do any good. Everything tipped sideways. It felt like we were on the deck of a sinking ship. The world twisted and blurred together.

That was when the platform dropped away.

I must've lost consciousness for a second or two. Probably better that way. I doubt I would've enjoyed being awake when I fell thirty feet and landed in a pile of rubble and steel.

My brain was throbbing. My ribs felt as if they'd been pummeled by a runaway rhinoceros, but at least I was still alive. I pulled my leg out from beneath a crisscross of broken railing and saw Milton beside me, climbing out of a mountain of bent metal and destroyed computer equipment.

"Did you see what happened to Vex?" I asked.

"No. But we've got bigger problems." Milton pointed toward the neutralizing barrier.

As soon as I turned to look, a wave of horror swept over me. Vex must've reached the phone before the explosion, because white gas had begun pouring down from the ceiling above Sophie and Captain Justice.

A mass of twisted steel was piled up where the platform had collapsed. At the edge of the wreckage was the phone.

"Come on," I said to Milton. "We need to get that phone."

"What about Vex?" Milton asked.

I scanned the room. Burning canisters, heaps of broken metal. But no sign of Vex.

"He must've been crushed when the platform collapsed," I said.

Milton looked doubtful, but he followed me to where the phone was lying. I picked it up and jabbed the touch screen with my thumb. The screen lit up, looking like any other smartphone display. Rows and rows of little icons. Swiping my finger across the screen shifted the display to a bunch of new icons. An hourglass, an open door, a scorpion, a fist.

So at least the phone still worked—that was the good news. The bad news was that there were about a hundred different apps to choose from.

"One of these has to shut off the neutralizing shield," I said.

"Yeah, but . . ." Milton stared at the touch screen, the endless columns of apps. "How're we supposed to know which one it is?"

"No clue, but we'd better find it soon." I glanced back at the glowing barrier. The white fog had drifted lower. Sophie and Captain Justice were hunched close to the floor. It wouldn't be long before the poisonous cloud reached them.

"Okay." Milton took a deep breath, concentrating on the screen. Suddenly he pointed at one of the icons. The open door. "What about that one? It might have something to do with releasing them."

I brought my finger close to the screen—then hesitated. What if Milton was wrong? But we had no choice.

As soon as I pressed the screen, a hatch in the floor opened beneath my feet.

"Aaaaah!" I screamed, arms flailing as my body dropped into the emptiness below.

At the last possible second, I grabbed the edge of the floor. My feet kicked at the empty air beneath me.

Gasping, I glanced down. Below was a pit of spikes.

"So *that's* what the open door means?" Milton said, helping me out of the hole.

After what had just happened, I wasn't exactly thrilled about the idea of testing out all the other apps. But we didn't have any choice. I scrolled through the phone, my heart pounding like an out of control marching band. I picked one of the apps—a square with three bars inside.

"You might want to hold on to something," I warned Milton.

And then I pressed the button.

A metallic groan echoed through the room. Glancing toward the noise, I saw that the glass wall—the wall that contained all the supervillains—was lowering.

I selected the app right next to the one I'd just pushed—an image of what looked like handcuffs. As soon as I pressed the screen, the steel restraints that were holding all the villains opened. The villains collapsed to the floor.

So at least we'd released the villains. But Sophie and Captain Justice were no closer to safety.

"Here, let me try," Milton said.

He scrolled through the options before choosing three apps that were all in the same row. The first one opened a hole in the ceiling. The next caused a rocket to rise up out of the floor. And the third launched the rocket into the sky.

"Hmm . . ." Milton scratched his head. "That wasn't what I'd hoped for."

I tried an app at the bottom right corner of the screen. All of a sudden, a secret door opened at the far end of the room.

"Hey, great!" Milton screamed. "Once we free everyone, we can escape through that door!"

I pressed another app, causing the secret doorway to erupt in flames.

"Never mind," Milton said.

Desperation flooded my mind. The choices seemed endless. Behind the glowing barrier, Sophie and Captain Justice were flat on their stomachs, the fog of poisonous gas floating just above them. If we went on picking apps randomly, we'd never save them in time. We needed to find the right one—now.

I concentrated on the screen. Each picture offered a clue. The open door had caused the hatch to drop open under me. The handcuffs had released the metal clasps around the supervillains. But disabling a neutralizing shield? What kind of a picture was *that* supposed to be? And how would I ever know it when I saw it?

That was when one of the apps caught my eye. A logo.

My finger shot forward. I pressed the screen with so much force that I nearly knocked the phone right out of my hand.

The glowing barrier flickered and then vanished. At the same moment, the gas swept upward, toward the pipe where it had come from. I could hear the loud hum of a fan working, sucking the gas back up into the pipe.

My heart kicked with relief and fear. The glowing wall was gone. But Sophie and Captain Justice weren't moving.

Milton and I ran across the room. I dropped to the ground beside Sophie. Her eyes were closed. Her hair was spilled out across the steel floor beneath her.

"Sophie?" I said. "Are you okay? Can you hear me?"

All I could think about was how I'd ignored her back at school, how I'd accused her dad of controlling the smoke creatures when it had been Vex all along. I should've never gotten Sophie involved in all this. It was my fault she was there.

These thoughts were splintered by Milton's voice.

"He's alive!" he said.

Captain Justice lurched sideways, gripping his chest. His fingers flicked at the sides of the *J* logo on his uniform as he broke into a coughing fit.

And then Sophie was coughing too. She inhaled a deep breath, as if she'd just come up from underwater.

"Oh, Sophie!" Captain Justice said. "You're alive!"

"Dad!" Sophie's voice was weak. She swung an arm around his shoulder. When she opened her eyes again, she looked at me. "You rescued us!" she said.

"Yeah, well," I muttered awkwardly. "I just sort of messed with the phone until something happened—"

I stopped talking when Sophie's arms wrapped around me. She squeezed me tightly. For a moment, I forgot about the mounds of crushed steel and rubble all around, the explosions and deadly fireballs flying through the air above us. She released me, then gave Milton a hug too.

"I knew you guys would figure something out!" she said.

"My gratitude goes out to you!" Captain Justice said. "To you both."

Milton blushed when Captain Justice glanced at him. I half expected him to ask for another autograph. Instead, a voice rose up behind me.

"Sorry to break up such a nice reunion."

I turned around. Vex was standing in a pile of destroyed machinery.

25

Although Phineas Vex doesn't actually possess any superpowers, he has shown over the years that he is an extremely skilled villain.

He looked like something out of a nightmare.

A grisly cut ran across one side of his face, forming a jagged *T* with the scar that was already there. His hands were dark with burns. His eye patch had been ripped away, revealing an unseeing white eye underneath.

Vex grabbed Sophie by the shoulder. The deadly handle of his cane was pointed at her head. Taking one step back, he dragged Sophie with him.

"If anyone moves, I'll kill her," he said.

Captain Justice's shoulder flexed. He looked like

every muscle in his body was ready to lunge forward. But Vex shoved the skull closer to Sophie's head, his eyes flashing. This put a stop to anything Captain Justice might've been planning to do.

"Stay where you are and I'll let her live," Vex said. Fire flickered against his skin. His one good eye swung wildly across each of us. The other eye remained perfectly still, like a white marble in his head. "It would be a shame for me to kill your wife *and* your daughter."

The sound of these words sent a shudder down my spine. Sophie's mom was dead. And Vex was the one who'd killed her.

"I'm taking the girl with me," Vex said. "If I see anyone following me, she dies. When I get to my destination, I'll let her go."

Behind Vex, a few of the villains were beginning to move, white robes shifting on the floor. One of them staggered to his feet, and I caught sight of his face. My dad. He swayed unsteadily, then took a few steps in our direction.

Vex dragged Sophie to a control panel built into the wall. Gripping Sophie with one hand, he reached out with the other and punched a few buttons. The wall slid sideways, revealing a hover SUV resting on a launchpad.

Behind him, Dad stumbled closer. Watching him, I feared what my dad would do. I knew how much he admired Vex, and how much he hated Captain Justice. Was he planning to help Sophie? Or Vex?

Then his eyes flickered over to me, and I knew whose side he was on.

Reaching forward with both hands, Dad grabbed hold of Vex's cane and yanked it away from Sophie's head. Vex spun around, growling with anger and surprise. Dad tried to keep hold of the cane, but Vex overpowered him. In the next instant, Vex had the cane in his grip again. He was aiming it at my dad's chest.

The skull's eyes glowed red. I watched it all happening as a horrible understanding dawned on me. Vex was going to kill my dad. There was nothing I could do. There was nothing any of us could do.

But that didn't stop me from trying. Flinging out my hands, I lunged forward. A surge of power rippled across my entire body.

And then everything just . . .

Stopped.

Or at least, that was the way it seemed. The scene in front of me was like a photograph. My vision focused on Vex, and from my hands a wave of light appeared.

Even as I watched it happen, I didn't believe it. A ribbon of pure, white light traced from the tips of my fingers into the air in front of me. I had the feeling I couldn't have stopped it even if I'd wanted to. It was as though I weren't the one controlling the power, but the other way around.

The power was controlling me.

When the light reached Vex, time started up again. Sound poured into my ears. Everything burst into motion. A sudden jolt hit me like a train, knocking me off my feet and propelling me backward.

The last thing I saw before my feet left the ground was Vex. The light must've had the same effect on him, because he went flinging in the opposite direction. He lost his grip on Sophie and went catapulting backward into a metal column. The force of the impact was enough to knock the column loose, along with the section of the ceiling it was supporting. The ceiling collapsed, burying Vex in a mountain of steel and stone.

I slammed into the ground. My lungs ached. My brain felt like it had been dropped into a blender and set on frappé. A blurry figure approached, speaking to me in Milton's voice.

"Are you okay?" he asked.

"Yeah. I think so."

Milton was suddenly talking very quickly, his voice rattling in my ear. "Man, that thing you did with the light. That was awesome! And the way you catapulted backward. I've never seen anything like it—"

"Sophie," I interrupted. "Is she all right?"

"I'm fine," came Sophie's voice. "Your dad's okay too."

"And my mom?" I turned, trying to spot her among all the fuzzy shapes in the distance. "Is she—"

"We can talk more once we're outside!" Captain Justice's voice called out. He brought a hand down on Sophie's shoulder. "But for now we need to get out of here. This entire room is going to collapse."

Captain Justice had a point. Climbing to my feet, I glanced up just in time to see another huge section of the ceiling falling away. It landed on the ground just a few feet from where the white-robed villains were lying.

"What about them?" Sophie pointed to the group of villains. The rest of them were awake by now. They climbed to their feet, looking around at the burning chaos like they'd just entered a bad dream. "We can't leave them here."

Captain Justice stared at the group, unable to hide his disgust. The ground shook. More of the ceiling crumbled to the ground, falling perilously close to several semiconscious villains.

"Dad," Sophie said. "Please."

Captain Justice heaved a sigh. "Fine," he said. "I'll see what I can do." He pointed his hand upward. "Engage Protective Umbrella of Virtue!"

A blue holographic umbrella emerged from his wristband. It looked like the kind of thing you'd see on a beach, except a whole lot bigger. Enormous chunks of

226

stone and steel fell from above, but then stopped in mid-air when they made contact with the umbrella. The villains looked up, amazed.

"Okay, everybody," Captain Justice announced in an unenthusiastic voice. "An emergency exit is located next to the launchpad. Please make your way out of the underground lair in a quick and orderly fashion."

The villains began to stagger dazedly toward us. I caught sight of my mom among the group.

"Mom!"

I ran to meet her. With Milton and me on each side, we helped her across the room. When she reached Dad, they fell into each other's arms.

"Ahem. The Protective Umbrella of Virtue won't last forever," Captain Justice called out. "I suggest everyone evacuate the underground lair as soon as possible."

It was definitely one of the strangest things I'd ever seen: A hundred of the world's most dangerous villains stumbling in the same direction, all wearing identical white robes and looking confusedly at the collapsing lair and the giant holographic beach umbrella overhead, as Captain Justice ushered them toward the exit.

26

No matter how much you practice, you may never fully understand your power.

By the time the Carrolshire Fire Department arrived, the Ocean View Hotel had completely burned to the ground.

"Nice job today," the chief of police said to Captain Justice. "But I don't know if there's room in the jail for everyone." He gestured to the group of confused-looking villains standing nearby. "We might be able to bus them over to the federal prison. It's only about thirty miles away from—"

"That won't be necessary," Captain Justice said.

"They're free to go." He winced as he spoke, as if it caused him physical pain to say the words.

"But, Captain Justice," the chief said, "you've got some of the world's baddest bad guys out here. You can't just let them go."

Captain Justice sighed. "They didn't do anything wrong. Not this time, at least."

"Yeah, but it's only a matter of time until they're out on the streets, wreaking havoc again."

"I know. And when that time comes, I'll be there." Captain Justice looked up at the sky. "Worry not, human law enforcement officer. I shall be there—when evil rears its ugly head, when the world cries out for help, when—"

"*Okay*, we get the point." Sophie rolled her eyes.

The chief shrugged, then used his walkie-talkie to contact the rest of the police force. The villains were free to go.

Gradually the villains regained their senses. Most of them wandered into downtown Carrolshire in their flowing white robes, looking for rides home and freaking out the locals.

It felt like days had passed since my friends and I had first set out that morning for Carrolshire, but it was only early evening. The sun was hanging low in the sky. Heat from the burning hotel cut through the October chill like a gigantic campfire.

My mom brought her hands to rest on my shoulders.

"What you did back there was so brave," she said. "We couldn't be more proud of you."

"It wasn't such a big deal," I said. "If Dad hadn't snuck up on Vex like that, I doubt any of us would've survived."

Dad twisted at the sleeve of his robe and looked away. I could see the conflict on his face. For years, he had admired Phineas Vex. And now Vex was buried somewhere under the smoking mountain of rubble where the hotel used to be. This was just one more confusing event in a day full of confusing events. In the past twenty-four hours, my parents had been attacked by smoke creatures, teleported to an abandoned hotel, dressed up like giant babies, and rescued by their greatest opponent.

It had been a pretty weird day.

"I just stepped forward at the right moment," Dad said to me quietly. "You were the one who made all the difference."

I glanced back at the burning building we'd barely escaped. "I don't even know *what* I did. Something happened back there. I've never done anything like that before. It was like . . ." I searched for the right words to describe what had happened. The tide of light shooting out of my fingertips, time standing still. "It was like my Gyft took over."

"You remember what we said to you? On the night we told you about your Gyft?" The glow from the nearby fire flickered across my mom's features. "We told you that you're Gyfted beyond anything we've ever seen before. You have an extraordinary power, Joshua. But that power is volatile. There may be times when it seems as if you aren't in control of your Gyft, when it seems almost as if—"

"As if it's in control of me," I said.

Mom nodded, a steady look in her eyes.

I turned away from her, staring down at the gravel around my feet.

"Cheer up, Son," Dad said, jostling me by the shoulder. "You saved the day, remember? Without you, we'd probably all be buried under that." He pointed at the heap of flaming rubble nearby. "You should be proud of yourself."

No matter what he said, I still felt uncertainty kicking around inside my chest. What would happen the next time I lost control of my power, or the time after that?

My mood lifted a few minutes later when I glanced over and saw Sophie and Milton in the crowd. They squeezed between a group of firefighters and walked toward us.

"Hello, Milton," Dad said.

Milton stared at my parents like he'd just forgotten how to speak. All this time, he'd known them as my mom and dad—two ordinary grown-ups who lived down the street. And now here they were, the Dread Duo, standing right in front of him. It probably didn't help that they were wearing matching white gowns.

"I'm sure this comes as a bit of a shock," Mom said. "We would've told you sooner, but, well, secrecy is a necessary part of our job."

"Er—that's okay," Milton stuttered. "At least now I know why I'm never invited over to Joshua's house."

Mom and Dad both laughed at this. But their laughter died away as soon as their eyes moved to where Sophie was standing. Dad stared at her the way he looked at microorganisms he was studying in his lab. Mom crossed her arms and did her best impression of a stern professor.

"Mom, Dad," I began, "this is Sophie—Sophie Justice. She's my—uh, project partner in class." I looked from my parents to her. "And my friend."

My parents examined Sophie in their unwelcoming way for a little longer, and then a polite smile finally showed on their faces. I guess after everything else they'd been through over the past twenty-four hours, nothing could shock them anymore. The three of them shook hands. I looked on, hoping my parents wouldn't do anything too embarrassing or life-threatening.

"It's nice to meet you, Sophie," Dad said.

"You did a great job back there," Mom added, glancing from Sophie to Milton. "Both of you. We can't thank you enough for coming here to rescue us."

"I'm just glad everyone's okay," Sophie said. "And you should've seen Joshua. The way he stood up to Vex back there. You would've been impressed."

I could feel my parents gazing proudly at me. I caught a glimpse of Sophie's smile.

"Well," Dad said, "we might go see if we can help out a few of our . . . er—colleagues. Some of them seem to be having a little difficulty coming out of their comatose states."

He pointed to a couple of white-robed supervillains who were trying to pick a fight with a telephone pole.

"Taste my wrath, you do-gooding nincompoop!" one of them said to the pole. The other attempted a karate chop and instead flopped onto the ground.

Once my parents had headed off in the direction of the confused villains, I turned to Milton. "You saved my life back there. You really *are* a superhero."

Milton shrugged like it was no big deal, but I could tell from his smile that he was secretly excited about the compliment.

By now, the Ocean View Hotel was nothing more than a smoldering pit. Firefighters sprayed the few sparse flames that were still burning.

"Do you have any idea what happened to my dad's car?" Sophie asked.

"What do you mean? It's right—" I pointed to where the red convertible had been parked when we'd arrived. In its place was an enormous crater. The only evidence that the car had ever been there was a charred license plate lying nearby. It had been split into two pieces. One half read JUST and the other, ICE.

"Your d-dad's car," Milton stuttered, "got blown up?"

"Apparently so." Sophie scratched her head, gazing at the crater questioningly. "Any idea how that might've happened?"

All of a sudden, I thought about the rocket we'd accidentally launched while randomly choosing apps on the cell phone. It definitely could've caused a crater like this.

"Nope," I said. "No idea."

"So, anyway, my dad made a call and had Stanley reprogrammed so he can come pick us up in the SUV. And . . ." Sophie paused. "And he invited you and your parents to come along too."

I stared at Sophie, hardly able to believe what I was hearing. "You think *my* parents should carpool with *your* dad?"

"After what they just went through, it beats the heck out of flying all the way back on hover scooters. Especially the way they're dressed." Sophie gestured toward my parents in their flowing robes. "I bet the wind gets pretty chilly at night. Besides, we're all going to the same place."

I wasn't sure how my parents would feel about sharing a ride with their greatest enemy.

On the other hand, a ride home *would* be nice.

27

The super community is smaller than it seems. Sooner or later, everyone gets to know everyone else.

So that was how the Dread Duo ended up sharing an armored SUV with Captain Justice and his daughter (not to mention me, Milton, and a robotic butler).

With the hover scooters strapped to the roof, the SUV pulled onto the highway.

"Shall I switch to hover mode, Mr. Justice?" Stanley asked, looking back at us from the front seat.

"Let's just keep it on the road, Stanley," Captain Justice said. "Better not to draw too much attention to ourselves."

Stanley nodded, and the SUV continued on. We drove for a long time in uncomfortable silence. I could tell that nobody knew quite what to say. It had been only a couple of weeks since Captain Justice had stopped my parents from destroying the world. Not to mention all the times in the past when they'd shot at, insulted, threatened, captured, and tried to kill each other.

But in the underground lair, they'd worked together to stop Vex. And now nobody quite knew *what* their status was, if they would go back to being hated enemies who tried to kill each other every few months . . . or if they now had a different kind of relationship. How exactly were they supposed to treat each other in the future?

Basically, it was awkward.

"That thing Vex said earlier about your mom," I said to Sophie. "Was he . . ."

I stopped speaking when I saw the way Sophie's expression had changed. All at once, I knew I'd stumbled onto the wrong topic. "I'm sorry," I said. "I shouldn't have—"

"It's okay," she said. "I can talk about it."

Her head was turned toward me, but she wasn't looking *at* me. Instead, her eyes seemed to be watching the scenery pass in the window.

"Sometimes I wake up at night and it's like it was only yesterday that I was out in the backyard with my mom, taking photographs of bugs. Other times, I feel like—like I can't remember anything about her at all."

She took a deep breath.

"My mom was a photographer," she said. "She worked for magazines, newspapers. She traveled a lot. Europe, South America, LA. My parents were never home at the same time. Either my mom was on assignment or my dad was out saving the world. For my tenth birthday, my mom took a little time off, and the three of us went skiing in Colorado. When we got back home, she was supposed to fly back to her assignment. But she called the magazine and convinced them to give her an extra couple of days so we could all be together, at least a little longer."

Sophie shook her head slowly, her eyes still focused on the window.

"The next day, she was supposed to pick me up from school, but she never showed up. Later I found out why. Someone had planted a bomb in the car." Sophie exhaled. "She died before she even made it out of the driveway. . . ."

Her voice trailed away.

"My dad eventually tracked the murder back to Vex," she said, after a long pause. "He did it to intimidate my dad, to make a point. I guess it's the same thing he was trying to do to me with those Firebottomed Rompers."

I thought about the armored SUV that we were riding

in, the bodyguard robot, the machine gun towers. It was all to protect Sophie. And even after all that, Vex had nearly gotten to her anyway.

"Ever since my mom died," Sophie said, "my dad's been following Vex. That's part of the reason why we were always moving around. My dad traced Vex across the country, and we moved from town to town every time he tracked Vex to a new location. A couple of months ago he found evidence that Vex was working on something in Sheepsdale. Something huge."

"So *that's* why you moved to Sheepsdale."

I felt a note of relief. Captain Justice wasn't there to drive my parents out of town. And now that they were carpooling together, who knew what would happen between them?

"Does this mean you won't have to move around anymore?" I asked hopefully. "You and your dad can stay in Sheepsdale now that Vex is dead, right?"

Sophie's mouth turned into a thoughtful frown. "What makes you think Vex is dead?"

"Um, let's see . . . A ton of metal and stone fell on top of him. And then he got buried underneath a burning building. I'd say there's a pretty good chance he's a goner."

"But you never *saw* him die."

"Well, no. But . . ." I could feel my confidence sinking. "Even if Vex *did* survive somehow, that hotel was surrounded by police and firefighters. They'd find him and arrest him before he could go anywhere."

Sophie's eyes stayed fixed on the window. I could tell she couldn't get Vex out of her head.

In front of us, my parents were trying to make conversation with Captain Justice.

"Those hologram weapons of yours are quite interesting," Dad said.

"Oh, thank you," Captain Justice said.

"Do you make them yourself?" Mom asked.

"No, no. An engineering firm in California designs them for me. And then the wristbands are assembled in China. After that, my public relations department comes up with the name."

"Well, they certainly do seem to come in handy," Dad said. "We would've all been crushed back there if it weren't for that Protective Umbrella of Honor."

"Virtue," Captain Justice said.

"Pardon?"

"You would've been crushed if it weren't for the Protective Umbrella of *Virtue*."

"Right," Dad said. "Of course."

Captain Justice cleared his throat. "Yes, well . . . these wristbands have helped me out of many a jam. Though, I must say, I've always admired your technology too. That Deactomatic of yours. Truly innovative. Is it something that you purchased?"

"Actually, that's one of my own inventions." Dad glanced away, trying not to smile.

Mom placed a hand on Dad's knee. "He invents most of the technology that we use."

"Really!" Captain Justice looked genuinely impressed. "I don't see how you find the time."

"A lot of late nights in the garage," Mom confessed.

"And who takes care of the zombies?" Captain Justice asked. "Because I've noticed on more than one occasion how well trained they are."

"I suppose that's mostly my responsibility," Mom said.

"It's *entirely* her responsibility," Dad confided. "I just try to stay out of the way."

"Well, take my word for it," Captain Justice said, "most zombies are *far* less disciplined. The last time I battled the Abominator, his zombies were all so poorly trained and unorganized. Half of them didn't even *try* to eat my brain."

I couldn't believe what I was witnessing. They actually seemed to be having a normal conversation—or normal for them, at least—without a single insult or death threat. I guess it shouldn't have been too terribly surprising. They actually had a lot in common. It was just that in the past, they'd always been too busy trying to kill each other to sit down and talk like civilized human beings.

I tried to imagine the three of them getting together

again at some point under less crazy circumstances. Maybe a cup of coffee or dinner somewhere. If they took off their uniforms and avoided the past— Would something like that be possible? It seemed pretty unlikely. Then again, it had also seemed unlikely that my parents would ever be in the same car as Captain Justice in the first place.

But there we were.

28

Keeping a secret identity can add a whole new level of complication to your life. But for many within the super community, there's no other choice.

I was almost happy to return to school on Monday. After the crazy couple of weeks I'd just lived through, it was a relief to get back into a normal routine.

At home, my dad was working on a new invention, the No Handz WonderGroom, a machine that brushed your hair for you. He'd even tested it out on himself the night before.

"I think it still needs a little work," he'd said afterward, carefully touching the brand-new bald spot on the side of his head.

Mom spent all of Sunday driving around Sheepsdale,

rounding up the zombies who'd gone missing after the Dread Duo's operation at ChemiCo Labs had gone awry. Most of them had broken into the health food store that was just down the highway from the lab. They'd eaten their way through the entire inventory of tofu by the time my mom had gotten there.

"Just one more on the loose," Mom said, pouring a jug of water into Micus's pot. The houseplant flapped his branches up and down appreciatively. "But I'm sure it'll turn up eventually."

One thing my parents didn't mention was the ride home they'd shared with Captain Justice. I couldn't help wondering what would happen the next time the three of them ran into each other. With my parents, it was only a matter of time before they got themselves involved in some kind of plot for world domination or destruction. Whenever that happened, Captain Justice was sure to show up eventually. And now that they'd been carpool buddies, it might be a little awkward to go back to trying to kill each other.

At school, I was having even more trouble than usual concentrating during class. My thoughts kept turning back to those last fiery moments in the lair. The way time had stopped. The string of light that had appeared from my fingertips. The jolt that had knocked me backward and had done the same to Vex.

You're Gyfted beyond anything we've ever seen before, Mom

had said. *You have an extraordinary power, Joshua. But that power is volatile.*

As annoying and unpredictable as my spontaneous combustion could be, I guess I didn't have much choice but to live with it. And I had to admit, it *had* come in handy.

No matter how I tried to put Vex out of my mind, he kept burning through my thoughts. It seemed impossible that he was still alive. But if he was, I knew he would make it his personal mission to come after us. And if that time came, my friends and I would have to be ready.

When lunch rolled around, Milton and I took our seats at our usual table. Just looking down at the food on my tray caused my appetite to shrivel. It was Meat Surprise Monday in the cafeteria. They called it a surprise because—well, nobody knew *what* it was.

After scooping a little of the brown mush onto my fork, I tried to stomach a bite. The meat was definitely surprising. And not in a good way.

"Guess what," Milton said, taking a bite of his sandwich. "James Wendler said he'd give me his chocolate milk for the rest of the year if I let him have the copy of *Super Scoop* that Captain Justice autographed."

"I doubt your mom would be okay with that," I pointed out.

"Yeah, but . . ." Milton's eyes went all dreamy for a second. "So much chocolate milk . . ." He took another bite. "Besides, Sophie can always get me another auto-graph."

"You really think she'd do that?"

"Why not? Captain Justice is her—"

Milton stopped talking when he noticed the sharp look I was giving him.

He'd been this way all day. Almost blabbing the truth in the middle of a crowded hallway or making mysterious comments that only we would understand. Unlike Sophie and me, Milton wasn't used to keeping so many secrets. And the effort seemed to be taking its toll.

"Maybe you're right," Milton said now. "A Captain Justice autograph is worth more than just one chocolate milk per day."

"That actually wasn't the point I was trying to—"

"I bet I could talk James up to a chocolate milk *and* an ice cream sandwich."

The conversation came to a halt when a wave of perfume rolled past. A second later, the Cafeteria Girls took their usual seats at the table. They were all wearing pink. The one sitting closest to me had on a pink camouflage outfit, as if she were planning on hiding out in a jungle made of bubble gum.

"So I figured it out," she announced.

"Figured *what* out?" asked one of her color-coordinated friends.

"Who Sophie Smith *really* is."

This got everyone's attention. Including mine.

"Sophie Smith is hiding her identity," Commando Barbie said.

"She is?"

"That's right. And I know why."

I nearly blurted out, *You do?* Luckily, the other Cafeteria Girls said it before I had a chance.

Pink Camo Pants nodded. Her eyes moved around the table. They passed over Milton and me quickly with an expression that said *Eww*.

"Remember when Sophie first showed up in Sheepsdale?" she said. "It was the day after Captain Justice had that big fight with the Dread Duo. That couldn't just be a coincidence."

My stomach lurched, and I had a feeling it wasn't the Meat Surprise. It sounded like the girls were actually on the right track. I already knew what would happen if people around town started figuring out Sophie's real identity. I'd been through it enough times myself. There'd be a sudden move. A new town, a new name, a new life.

And Sophie would be gone.

I'll admit, I hadn't known her all that long, and for at least part of that time we'd been mad at each other or ignoring each other, or both. But we'd been through a lot together. Something about surviving a few near-death experiences with someone makes you feel close to them.

I guess what I'm trying to say is, I didn't want to see her leave.

The girl in the hot pink camouflage said, "There's a reason why Sophie Smith just happened to show up in Sheepsdale the day after the Dread Duo were battling it out downtown. Isn't it obvious?"

Everyone at the table waited for her to go on. I was clasping the edge of the table nervously. Milton was so distracted that he'd eaten his way through his entire sandwich and was now chewing on the plastic Baggie it had come in.

"Sophie's parents are the Dread Duo," Commando Barbie said.

I nearly burst into laughter. Sophie's secret was still safe. And apparently mine was too.

"Wait a second . . . ," said another girl. "How could Sophie's mom be the Botanist? I thought she didn't even *have* a mom."

"Duh," said Pink Camo Pants. "They're trying to keep it a secret."

"Oh."

"Think about it. The machine gun towers outside their house, the torture devices. Her mom and dad are super-villains."

Silence settled over the table as the other girls thought about what they'd just learned. They looked like they actually believed it too. And then, all at once, their eyes went wide with horror. I glanced over my shoulder and instantly recognized what had frightened them.

Sophie was standing next to our table.

"Do you mind if I sit here?" she asked the Cafeteria Girls, pointing at an empty seat.

For the first time ever, the Cafeteria Girls were speechless. They stared back at Sophie in shocked silence. They had the same terrified expressions that people got whenever my parents showed up somewhere. Except those people weren't usually dressed all in pink.

"Uh . . . ," Commando Barbie managed to say.

"Thanks!" Sophie smiled sweetly at the girls, then dropped into a seat beside them. She looked over at me, and I saw a mischievous glimmer flash in her eyes. Then she turned her attention back to the Cafeteria Girls. "Would any of you happen to have an extra set of silverware I could borrow?" she asked in her most polite voice.

All four of the Cafeteria Girls gawked back at Sophie like she'd just asked if she could borrow a grenade launcher. Pink Camo Pants elbowed the girl nearest her, nodding at an unused fork and knife on her tray.

"H-here," said the girl. She held out the silverware in two shaking hands.

Sophie took the offering. Still smiling, she squeezed the fork and knife in her fist. The Cafeteria Girls winced at the sound of metal grinding against metal.

"You know what?" Sophie said. "I just realized I don't need any silverware after all. You can have this back."

Sophie opened her hand, and a lump of twisted metal dropped onto the table with a thud. The Cafeteria Girls had gone as pale as four pink-clad ghosts.

"And if I find out you're talking about me behind my back again, it won't just be the silverware that gets damaged," Sophie whispered. "Do I make myself clear?"

The innocent smile was gone. Sophie's skin was shining with a faint glow—not so bright that it would be noticed by anyone else in the cafeteria, but definitely enough to get her point across. The Cafeteria Girls looked like they were about ready to jump out of their own skins. Pink Camo Pants was so freaked out that she didn't even notice when a chunk of Meat Surprise slid off the table and into her lap.

"That oughta shut them up for a while," I said a few minutes later as we stepped out of the cafeteria and into the courtyard.

"I don't know how much good it'll do." Sophie shrugged. "My dad usually finds a way to reveal our secret sooner or later. I'm just sick of pretending I don't know that everyone's talking about me."

It was one of the last warm days of the year. Soon winter would sweep through Sheepsdale and blanket the courtyard with snow. But for now kids were using the space to eat their lunches and hang out with friends, playing four square and wall ball.

Over by the tetherball pole, I spotted Joey and Brick. Ever since their little confrontation with Sophie outside the girls' restroom, they'd avoided us. Now they spent most of their time picking on kids who were so small or nerdy that they'd never put up a fight.

At the moment, Brick had a fifth grader by the collar. Joey was standing next to him. His arm was still cradled inside a sling, but that didn't prevent him from giving orders.

"Hold him tight," he said to Brick.

Brick yanked the fifth grader backward.

They'd done this with me before too—ripping the ball loose and then tying my ankle to the end of the tetherball rope. With me hanging upside down, Brick and Joey had knocked me back and forth.

Tether-Joshua.

And now they were about to do it to someone else.

Sophie and I stepped forward at the same time. But before either of us could say anything, the kid caught sight of something that was even more frightening than Joey and Brick. His jaw dropped, and he pointed one trembling finger at what he'd just seen.

A zombie had entered the courtyard.

29

**In the end, only you can choose whether
to become a hero, a villain,
or something in between.**

At least now we knew what had happened to the
last of my parents' missing zombies. It looked
like it had gone on a looting spree. The zombie was wearing a flower-print Hawaiian shirt and a pair of khaki
slacks. On one foot it had on an oversized snow boot and
on the other was a sandal, as if it couldn't decide whether
to dress for snow or the beach. Its wrists were cluttered
with silver and gold bracelets. And on its head was a
cowboy hat and a pair of aviator sunglasses.

It was definitely the weirdest-looking zombie I'd ever
seen. And that was saying something.

The courtyard cleared out in a flash as kids escaped in every direction. With their backs turned on the zombie, Joey and Brick were oblivious. Besides, they were used to kids running away screaming whenever they were nearby.

The fifth grader's voice cracked as he pointed across the courtyard. "Z-zombie," he said. "It's coming."

Brick let out a dry laugh. "Yeah, right," he said. "We're not falling for that."

"Next you're gonna tell us elephants are stampeding through school, right?" Joey said.

They stopped joking when the zombie let out a low growl. I'd heard a similar noise coming through the floorboards of our house many times before. It was a zombie's way of saying, "I'm hungry."

Joey and Brick turned in the direction the growl had come from. When Brick saw what was behind him, he released his grip on the fifth grader. The kid went running out of sight, but Joey and Brick were frozen with fear. The zombie took two staggering steps toward them.

"Do you think we should do something?" Sophie asked in a dull voice.

"I don't know," I said. "I think I might enjoy watching Joey get his brain eaten."

"And Brick doesn't have a brain to eat," Milton added.

As much as I didn't like the idea of helping Joey and Brick, I knew my parents would get blamed if anything happened to them.

Next to us was a big rubber ball someone had abandoned halfway through a game of four square. I tossed it across the courtyard. The zombie watched as it bounced across the cement and rolled into a bush. It wasn't much of a distraction, but it bought Joey and Brick enough time to get a head start across the courtyard.

"Make sure all the doors are locked," I said once Joey and Brick had made it to safety. "I'll find something to keep the zombie busy until my parents can get here to pick it up."

"Like what?" Milton demanded.

I glanced back through the glass doors behind us. "I have an idea."

While Sophie and Milton secured the doors, I sprinted through the cafeteria. Principal Sloane's voice boomed over the intercom. "Witnesses have reported a possible zombie sighting. All students and staff should carry out the appropriate procedure at once."

We'd practiced the zombie drill a few times over the past couple of years, but this was the first time the school was doing it for real. Basically, it was the same thing as the tornado drill and the Dread-Duo-have-unleashed-a-mudslide-and-it's-headed-our-way drill. Everyone crouched under their desks. And in the case of zombies, the teacher ensured that the door was locked.

Weaving between crowds of panicked students, I bolted through the cafeteria. The lunch ladies were crouched beneath tables. One of them screamed, raising her spatula like a sword. When she realized I wasn't a zombie, her expression shifted to confusion.

"If you want seconds, you'll have to come back later!" she barked.

"That's not why I'm here." I pushed through the waist-high swinging doors that led into the kitchen. "I came to get—*that*."

A big pot of Meat Surprise was resting on top of the stove. After grabbing a pair of oven mitts off the floor, I lifted the pot and carried it back through the cafeteria.

I paused for a second when I reached the doors that opened out onto the courtyard. Through the glass, I saw the zombie, looking like a Hawaiian cowboy with a taste for expensive jewelry. It was holding a wooden bench over its shoulder and was staggering toward a row of windows. I didn't want to imagine what would happen if it broke through a window and got inside one of the classrooms.

Milton unlocked the door and I stepped outside, carrying the Meat Surprise with me.

"Hey, you!" I called.

The zombie turned to face me, and I felt a shiver run down my neck. No matter how many times I encountered them, making eye contact with zombies gave me the creeps.

I gulped down my fear and took a step forward.

"I brought something for ya!" I held up the pot of Meat Surprise.

The zombie dropped the bench it had been carrying. Licking its gray lips, it began to approach, moving more quickly with each step. I set the pot of Meat Surprise on the ground, then turned and got out of there before the zombie had a chance to make me its dessert.

Luckily, Sophie always carried her phone with her in case of emergency. And this definitely qualified as an emergency. I borrowed it to call my parents, who said they would get to the school as soon as possible. But watching the zombie through the glass doors, I wondered if that would be fast enough.

The zombie reached inside the pot and pulled out a handful of the brown mush. After taking a sniff, it made a disgusted face. Apparently, it wasn't a fan of the Meat Surprise either.

Within a few minutes, the zombie had lost all interest in what I'd given it. Wandering back across the courtyard, it picked up the bench again. If my parents didn't make it there soon, the zombie was going to cause some serious damage.

I wasn't too excited about the idea of fighting a zombie on my lunch break, but it was getting close to the window, and I didn't see any other way to stop it. I unlocked the door and stepped back into the courtyard. That was as far as I got, though.

Thanks to Pippa and Lola for keeping me company while I'm at work all day.

I can't begin to express how grateful I am to my family who support me in writing and everything else. The Greeks and Trulls: Stephen, Claudia, Amy, Lauren, Travis, and Caitlyn. The Sviens and Sissells: Doug, Sherilyn, Erin, Dennis, and Kim. The Owens: Mike, Carla, and Cody. Layla Price. Librarian extraordinaire and early reader Kristy Fowler Compton. My wonderful grandparents James and Sue Greek. *Und natürlich meine Familie auf der anderen Seite des Atlantiks:* Michael, Irmtrud, and Karin Schlör, as well as Zenta Englert. Evan Bacon, my bigger little brother, true friend, and occasional collaborator. And of course, my parents: Terry and Jamie Bacon, who have always inspired me to take over the world.

And finally, I want to thank my wife, Eva, for supporting me in all my schemes, evil and otherwise.

Just as the zombie raised the bench, preparing to swing, a noise ricocheted across the courtyard and a dart sprouted from the zombie's neck. It grasped at the dart with one of its gray hands, staggering around for a few seconds before dropping the bench and collapsing to the ground.

A second later, a pair of hover scooters descended below the rooftops and into the courtyard. Mom and Dad were in their uniforms, though I could tell they'd gotten dressed in a hurry, because Dad still had on his house slippers.

Mom holstered her tranquilizer gun and climbed off the hover scooter. Her eyes caught sight of me across the courtyard with a quick glimpse of recognition. Then she and Dad set to work.

The zombie was lying facedown in the grass, snoring loudly. Its cowboy hat and sunglasses were scattered a few feet away. While Mom lifted its legs, Dad tugged a net underneath, wrapping it around the zombie. He then attached the net to the bumpers of their hover scooters.

As she usually did after handling zombies, Mom removed a bottle of hand sanitizer from her utility belt and cleaned her hands, then shared the bottle with Dad. After that, they climbed onto their hover scooters. On the count of three, they pulled up on the handles and rose back into the air.

With the zombie hanging in its net beneath them,

Mom and Dad drifted upward until they vanished from sight.

It wasn't my parents' usual activity—saving a schoolful of kids from getting devoured by a zombie. And I have to admit I felt a little proud. For once, my mom and dad weren't the ones wreaking havoc. They were the ones making the world a little safer.

Of course, the zombie would never have made it into our school in the first place if it hadn't escaped from my parents.

But hey—nobody's perfect.

ACKNOWLEDGMENTS

Many thanks to Sarah Burnes, my agent, for the superb guidance and advocacy for this book, and Logan Garrison, for plucking my manuscript from the slush pile and sticking with it ever since. Also, my gratitude goes to Rebecca Gardner and Will Roberts, for bringing Joshua Dread out into the world, as well as to all the other wonderful folks at the Gernert Company.

I'm so thankful to Wendy Loggia, who spotted the book I wanted to write from the beginning and has done so much to guide me in that direction, as well as Beverly Horowitz, Krista Vitola, Trish Parcell, and everyone at Delacorte Press, for all the support you've provided along the way.

Thank you, Brandon Dorman; your cover was far better than I could've ever hoped.

Thank you, Miriam Berkley, for spending a breezy afternoon in Dumbo with me and taking a thousand photographs, including one that was printable.

I would like to thank Amy Gordon for reading the book more than once and offering the kind of feedback that can only come from a Kids' Book Expert. Thanks also to the other Kids' Book Pros and occasional ski buddies, Kalah McCaffrey and Christopher Lupo, as well as fellow authors and early readers Adam Gidwitz and Sandy London.

Thank you, Mary Pender-Coplan. I'm so glad your son laughed at all the right parts.

Just as the zombie raised the bench, preparing to swing, a noise ricocheted across the courtyard and a dart sprouted from the zombie's neck. It grasped at the dart with one of its gray hands, staggering around for a few seconds before dropping the bench and collapsing to the ground.

A second later, a pair of hover scooters descended below the rooftops and into the courtyard. Mom and Dad were in their uniforms, though I could tell they'd gotten dressed in a hurry, because Dad still had on his house slippers.

Mom holstered her tranquilizer gun and climbed off the hover scooter. Her eyes caught sight of me across the courtyard with a quick glimpse of recognition. Then she and Dad set to work.

The zombie was lying facedown in the grass, snoring loudly. Its cowboy hat and sunglasses were scattered a few feet away. While Mom lifted its legs, Dad tugged a net underneath, wrapping it around the zombie. He then attached the net to the bumpers of their hover scooters.

As she usually did after handling zombies, Mom removed a bottle of hand sanitizer from her utility belt and cleaned her hands, then shared the bottle with Dad. After that, they climbed onto their hover scooters. On the count of three, they pulled up on the handles and rose back into the air.

With the zombie hanging in its net beneath them,

Mom and Dad drifted upward until they vanished from sight.

It wasn't my parents' usual activity—saving a schoolful of kids from getting devoured by a zombie. And I have to admit I felt a little proud. For once, my mom and dad weren't the ones wreaking havoc. They were the ones making the world a little safer.

Of course, the zombie would never have made it into our school in the first place if it hadn't escaped from my parents.

But hey—nobody's perfect.

ACKNOWLEDGMENTS

Many thanks to Sarah Burnes, my agent, for the superb guidance and advocacy for this book, and Logan Garrison, for plucking my manuscript from the slush pile and sticking with it ever since. Also, my gratitude goes to Rebecca Gardner and Will Roberts, for bringing Joshua Dread out into the world, as well as to all the other wonderful folks at the Gernert Company.

I'm so thankful to Wendy Loggia, who spotted the book I wanted to write from the beginning and has done so much to guide me in that direction, as well as Beverly Horowitz, Krista Vitola, Trish Parcell, and everyone at Delacorte Press, for all the support you've provided along the way.

Thank you, Brandon Dorman; your cover was far better than I could've ever hoped.

Thank you, Miriam Berkley, for spending a breezy afternoon in Dumbo with me and taking a thousand photographs, including one that was printable.

I would like to thank Amy Gordon for reading the book more than once and offering the kind of feedback that can only come from a Kids' Book Expert. Thanks also to the other Kids' Book Pros and occasional ski buddies, Kalah McCaffrey and Christopher Lupo, as well as fellow authors and early readers Adam Gidwitz and Sandy London.

Thank you, Mary Pender-Coplan. I'm so glad your son laughed at all the right parts.

Thanks to Pippa and Lola for keeping me company while I'm at work all day.

I can't begin to express how grateful I am to my family, who support me in writing and everything else. The Greeks and Trulls: Stephen, Claudia, Amy, Lauren, Travis, and Caitlyn. The Sviens and Sissells: Doug, Sherilyn, Erin, Dennis, and Kim. The Owens: Mike, Carla, and Cody. Layla Price. Librarian extraordinaire and early reader Kristy Fowler Compton. My wonderful grandparents James and Sue Greek. *Und natürlich meine Familie auf der anderen Seite des Atlantiks:* Michael, Irmtrud, and Karin Schlör, as well as Zenta Englert. Evan Bacon, my bigger little brother, true friend, and occasional collaborator. And of course, my parents: Terry and Jamie Bacon, who have always inspired me to take over the world.

And finally, I want to thank my wife, Eva, for supporting me in all my schemes, evil and otherwise.

About the Author

LEE BACON grew up in Texas with parents who never once tried to destroy the world (at least, not that he knew of). He lives in Brooklyn. This is his first novel.

Continue the Adventure

The Nameless Hero

Coming Fall 2013

When I got to the bus stop, I unzipped my back-pack and pulled out the Sheepsdale Middle School yearbook. I'd received it yesterday, just like everyone else in school.

Opening the book, I flipped through until I found my picture. I was the skinny kid in the lower right-hand part of the page who looked like he'd just been stumped by a tough math question. My disheveled brown hair blended perfectly with a shadow in the background, making it look like I had a huge lopsided Afro.

Otherwise, it was a great picture.

There was a name printed beneath the photo, but it wasn't my name. At least, not my real name. Part of being the child of two notorious supervillains is that you've got to hide your identity. People still called me Joshua, but only a few people—my parents, Milton, Sophie—knew my actual last name was Dread.

It can be tough to live with a false identity, to switch your names the way other people switch shoes. But just like everything else in life, after a while, you get used to it. Soon you mostly forget that you were ever anyone else.

I closed the yearbook with a sharp crack and shoved it inside my backpack. As I did, a slip of paper fell out. It fluttered in the air for a second, then landed next to my foot. I bent down to pick it up.

The paper was small, about the size of a postcard. One side was blank. I was about to toss it in the trash can when I noticed what was printed on the other side:

YOU ARE THE CHOSEN.

I stared at the words, my mind spinning to make sense of them. *The chosen?* What was that supposed to mean?

I nearly dropped the slip of paper when I heard a voice behind me.

"Hey, Joshua."

I spun around and saw Milton. Tall and thin, with

sandy blond hair that never seemed to stay in place, Milton had been my closest friend ever since I moved in down the street from him nearly three years earlier. Even after learning that my parents were the Dread Duo, he still treated me the same as he had before. Well, pretty much the same. Every once in a while, he asked to borrow my dad's plasma gun.

"I've got big plans for our first week of summer," Milton said. "On Monday, we can go to AwesomeWorld. You know, that new amusement park outside town? They have a ride there that's so extreme, if you don't puke you get your money back!"

"That sounds . . . great," I said, hardly listening. My thoughts were still coiled around the slip of paper in my hand. *You are the chosen.* How could it have gotten into my backpack without me knowing? And what did it mean?

Chosen for *what*?

As the bus pulled up, I gripped the note a little tighter in my fist. All of a sudden, I had a feeling that my plans for a relaxing, stress-free summer had just gone up in flames.

Excerpt copyright © 2012 by Lee Bacon. Published by Delacorte Press, an imprint of Random House Children's Books, a division of Random House, Inc., New York.

OCT 2012

CLIFTON PARK-HALFMOON PUBLIC LIBRARY, NY

0 00 06 04023408